MONEY IN THE GRAVE 3

Lock Down Publications and Ca$h
Presents
MONEY IN THE GRAVE 3
A Novel by *Martell "Troublesome" Bolden*

Lock Down Publications
Po Box 944
Stockbridge, Ga 30281

Visit our website @
www.lockdownpublications.com

Lock Down Publications
Like our page on Facebook: Lock Down Publications @
www.facebook.com/lockdownpublications.ldp

Book interior design by: **Shawn Walker**
Edited by: **Shamika Smith**

Stay Connected with Us!

Text **LOCKDOWN** to 22828 to stay up-to-date with new releases, sneak peaks, contests and more...
Thank you.

Submission Guideline.

Submit the first three chapters of your completed manuscript to ldpsubmissions@gmail.com, subject line: Your book's title. The manuscript must be in a .doc file and sent as an attachment. Document should be in Times New Roman, double spaced and in size 12 font. Also, provide your synopsis and full contact information. If sending multiple submissions, they must each be in a separate email.

Have a story but no way to send it electronically? You can still submit to LDP/Ca$h Presents. Send in the first three chapters, written or typed, of your completed manuscript to:

LDP: Submissions Dept
Po Box 944
Stockbridge, Ga 30281

DO NOT send original manuscript. Must be a duplicate.

Provide your synopsis and a cover letter containing your full contact information.

Thanks for considering LDP and Ca$h Presents.

Martell "Troublesome" Bolden

CHAPTER 1

"So you mean to tell me that you murked Rob?"

"Yeah. I murked 'em all and kept movin'."

Inside of Swindle's duck-off spot, he and Bone sat on the couch in the front room discussing matters. Aside from the two of them, Vito was present also. Bone had gone directly to the duck-off to meet with Swindle in order to sell him the bricks that were obtained from the lick on Castle, which he had taken all for himself, along with the money. After betraying the gang and leaving them for dead back in the hotel room at the Diamond Inn, he didn't even have it on his mental. But Bone didn't realize just how detrimental his betrayal would be.

Swindle took a pull of the blunt of weed then said, "Now since you got rid of Rob, you can count up much more paper. And that's exactly why I got rid of Heavy."

"Good riddance," Bone scoffed. "Heavy and Rob was holdin' us back any-fuckin'-way."

"Now we won't have either of them niggas gettin' in the way of us doin' business."

"Speakin' of..." Bone grabbed the duffel bag from the floor near his feet and set it atop the coffee table. He unzipped the duffel bag, then began removing the individually packaged kilos of coke and stacked them one atop the other in two piles until all twelve were there. Afterwards, he zipped up the duffel, which also had the money inside, and replaced it on the floor at his feet then said, "Let's talk business."

Swindle grinned once he noticed that each kilo was stamped with the Libra logo. "I'm sure whatever you had to do for those bricks wasn't personal."

"It's never personal, always business," Bone told him "Now, those bricks are yours for a hunnit G's."

"How 'bout I give you fifty now and the other fifty after I make a flip," Swindle bargained.

"Cool. I'll expect the other fifty in a week, tops, or I'll be expectin' double that."

"It's like that, Bone?" He took a pull of the blunt, inhaling thick weed smoke into his lungs.

"It's business, remember?" Bone declared. He grabbed up the Mac-10 from his lap in one hand and the duffel from the floor in the other as he stood. "Now where's the paper?"

Swindle dug into the pockets of his Amiri jeans, then came out with two bankrolls and handed them over to Bone. "That's forty G's. Vito, why don't you give him another ten," Swindle instructed.

As instructed, Vito fished in the pocket of his Balmain jeans and presented the rest of the money. He then tossed Bone the stack of bills that was wrapped with a rubber band and amounted to ten grand. Without bothering to count out the cash, Bone just put it inside the duffel with the rest from the lick. He had plans to count up all of the cash once alone at his place.

"I'll be in touch with you in a week. Make sure you have the rest of my paper by then," Bone asserted.

"Don't trip, Bone, I'll make sure to have the rest of your paper. And it'll be with interest," Swindle assured as he dumped ashes from the tip of the blunt into the ashtray on the end table.

"One week, Swindle." Bone turned and exited the duck-off spot.

Vito locked the door behind Bone and suggested, "Why don't you just do the nigga, Bone, and take all of his shit."

"'Cause I need him to keep bringin' me dope for the low. Besides, I'm gettin' more outta the deal than I would even if I was to take the shit from him," Swindle explained.

"A'ight. Now what?" Vito moved over to the couch and took a seat.

"Now I need for you to get rid of Rich so I can move these bricks without any beef." Swindle picked up one of the blocks and thought about how he had had Don murked for some bricks with the same Libra logo. Though he had managed to get Don out of the way, there was still Rich. And Swindle realized that if he didn't kill Rich first, then Rich would definitely kill him. Once he got rid of Rich, then Swindle would be able to run the drug trade in the hood with no problems.

***

Meantime, light snow began falling as Bone made his way to the Lexus SUV. He slid behind the steering wheel and set the Mac-10 on his lap and the duffel bag on the passenger seat. Catching a glimpse of himself in the rearview mirror, Bone noticed some dried blood splatters painted on his face.

Right then Bone thought about his now dead comrades. He justified stabbing them in their backs because he felt like they had turned their backs on him while he was on lockdown. After he was the one who had gotten jammed up on the murder/robbery charges instead of any of the others, Bone felt like for the most part they had left him to fend for himself. Since he was too solid to snitch on them, instead he plotted the ultimate betrayal as revenge.

Once Bone had beaten the charges and returned to the streets, all he needed to do was keep the others unsuspecting of his ulterior motive while he awaited the right opportunity to go through with his plot. And TJ didn't make it easy with having suspicions of him, but the good thing there was Max at his defense, and Rob had been blinded by the idea of them being a gang again. Little did they know, Bone had his mind set on getting revenge.

Pushing the Lex down the street, Bone was on the way to his place, where he would count up the cash. He could feed his greed since he didn't have to break bread now that TJ, Max, and Rob were dead. It's no doubt that greed gives rise to deadly motives.

***

There was a thunderous knock at the front door of the apartment, and when Trina opened up, she found a bleeding Rob.

Once Rob had regained consciousness back in the hotel room, Rob blinked open his eyes and saw a pool of his blood on the floor and then immediately he had had a flashback of Bone pulling the trigger in his face. Not wanting to stick around long enough for first responders to arrive on the scene, Rob had grabbed up his weapon before making his way out of the hotel. Since Bone had also taken the vehicle along with the caper money, Rob was left to flee the scene on foot. He needed someplace to lay low, and he figured Trina's place would be best for him to stay out of harm's way.

"Oh, Rob, you're bleeding! Hurry inside!" Trina pulled Rob inside and helped him over to the couch, where he took a seat. "I'll call you an ambulance."

Rob grabbed her arm and grumbled, "No, don't."

"But you have a bullet wound in your face!" she cried.

"It's not as bad as it looks. I'll live," he assured her. The bullet may have been fatal had he not slowed its impact when attempting to cover up with his hands just as Bone had pulled the trigger. The bullet had pierced through his left hand and left bullet fragments imbedded in his face. Blood still wept from his bullet-wounded face, and the bullet hole in his hand hurt like hell. "Listen, Trina, I'll need you to grab some supplies and cleanse these wounds then bandage them."

"Okay. I'll see what I can find." Trina hurried to gather any supplies she had around her apartment that would be helpful with patching up Rob's wounds. She returned with what she could find then first began nursing his wounded hand and inquired, "What happened to you, Rob?"

"Bone betrayed me and the others," Rob told her with anger in his tone. He couldn't help but think back to seeing Max's lifeless body riddled with bullets. And then he thought about TJ being left for dead during the lick.

"What do you mean he betrayed you?" She swathed his hand in a bandage after using peroxide to cleanse its wound.

"I mean nothin' about the lick on Castle went exactly as planned. Not only was TJ killed durin' the lick, but Max was killed by Bone, who attempted to kill my ass also. I didn't realize Bone had his own damn plans to betray the gang and take the fuckin' money all for himself."

"Can't believe Bone was willing to betray you over money."

"But I'ma make sure his ass regret it."

"And what about Castle and his girl, are they dead, too?" She dreaded the answer.

"Castle is still alive, but the girl isn't. I had nothin' personally to do with her death, but I do regret that it was her instead of Castle," Rob said, remorseful.

Trina felt bad about Parker but she couldn't change what had happened. "I didn't want her to end up dead."

"She wasn't really the intended target, but that's how it go when it goes bad."

"I know. It's just—"

"Ahh, shit!" Rob winced in pain as she nursed his wounded jaw.

"Sorry." Using a pair of sterilized tweezers, Trina removed the bullet fragments from the flesh of his jaw, then cleansed the wound with peroxide before dressing it with a gauze. "There. Now you're all taken care of."

"Good thing I have you to take care of me," Rob told her. He knew going to Shanta was out of the question after she had learned that he had a part in murkin' Don. But he couldn't focus on that for the time being while he had to heal. "Look, I'll need to stay here while I heal up."

"Of course. You can stay as long as you need to heal."

"Just until I'm healed enough to go after Bone. His ass has another fuckin' thing comin' if he thinks I'm dead." Rob was sure that Bone thought he was left dead in the hotel room. He wouldn't let Bone get away with his treachery, so if it was the last thing Rob did, he would dead Bone.

Trina gingerly grabbed his wounded hand and said, "Rob, maybe you should just forget all about Bone and let him keep the money."

"And allow Bone to get away with betrayal? This isn't about the money for me, but I won't let him keep the money or his life."

"If it isn't about the money, then what is it about?"

Rob looked her in the eyes and answered, "It's about honor."

"You know better than anyone that there's no honor amongst jack-boys."

"Which is why it's death before dishonor," he declared.

"Rob, I just don't want trying to get rich be the reason you end up dying."

"At least I'll die happy if I die rich." Rob understood as the old adage goes, money can't buy happiness. But when a nigga is born broke, then he is always determined to get rich or die tryin'.

Trina shifted towards him and expressed, "Rob, I don't want to see you die because I love you."

"And I don't take your love for granted," he replied.

"Hope not."

Rob stood to his feet and said, "Look, I'ma go and wash myself in the shower." He needed to wash away all of the blood, sweat, and tears.

"How about I join you?" Trina offered.

"No. I need a moment alone to think," Rob told her. He turned and headed to the bathroom, leaving Trina alone with her own thoughts.

After evading death, Rob was determined to dead anyone who posed a threat to him. Not only would he have Bone gunning for his head, but Rich still had money on his head. For Rob, killing Bone was personal and killing Rich was just business. Either way, it was him or them. Rob was fueled by money and blood.

Martell "Troublesome" Bolden

CHAPTER 2

Seated around the kitchen table in the trap house, Rich hand counted the cash and T-Mac wrapped each stack with rubber bands while Danger tossed them into a Prada backpack. They were counting the gains after flippin' the last of their product, and thus far the count was upwards of seventy bands. They had run it up over time, but for now they were without a plug and needed to find themselves another one. Though they still had beef in the streets, money was still the motive.

"Shit," Rich cursed out of frustration. For the second time he had lost count of the money, so luckily the others were there keeping count also. "What's the count?"

"Sixty-eight Gs," T-Mac told him. He had peeped that there must be something else on Rich's mind other than money. "You can't seem to concentrate on the paper, so what's on your mind, cuz?"

Rich halted his count and looked his boys in their eyes. "What's on my mind is murder. I can't let Swindle or Rob get away with the pain and losses they caused us. Now Swindle got Vito gunnin' for me, and I'm sure Rob's waitin' on his turn."

"And I get the feelin' that since Swindle had somethin' to do with Don gettin' murked, then he was also the one who sent someone to murk C-note. Maybe he even sent the nigga Rob again," Danger added.

"Either way, both of them bitch-ass niggas gotta meet the reaper for what happened to Don and C-note," T-Mac input.

"And I can't forget about what happened to my mom. Somebody have to answer for it, even if it kills me," swore Rich.

"Only ones that are gonna be killed are our opps," Danger assured.

"No cap," T-Mac seconded. "Swindle and Rob's asses is good as dead."

"Fa sho'," Rich agreed.

Leaving Swindle and Rob dead was the only option. Rich knew that it was either him or them. And apparently neither Swindle nor Rob had a problem with killing him and whoever else they had to. So, Rich would do his all to see to it that they ended up dead.

Rich picked up a stack of blue strips and said, "Now let's get back to this paper."

T-Mac leaned back in his chair then said, "Rich, we can't continue our paper chase without any weight. We need to find another plug A-sap."

"I know. And we need one just like the nigga that Don was plugged with," Rich said.

"You mean the nigga Castle," Danger chimed in.

"Right, him. I'm sure Castle has enough weight to front us whatever we cop."

"Only problem is we don't know how to get in touch with Castle," T-Mac pointed out.

Danger leaned forward, resting his elbows atop the table. "I know how we can get in touch with the nigga. There's this hookah lounge that Castle hang out at where he had Don meet with him at a couple times."

"Then we'll pull up to the lounge so me and Castle can talk money. I'll approach him with the same proposition as Don's. That way the nigga won't have a problem pluggin' me," Rich said. He understood that as long as he made Castle feel comfortable with the terms, then it would be in his best interest.

***

The Bentley SUV yielded to a halt at a stoplight. Two goons occupied the front seats with heavy artillery laying across their laps while Castle, alongside his right hand man, Sheik, took up the back. It was a cold night out as Castle and Sheik were on their way to the hookah lounge, which they frequented nearly every weekend. Ever since the lick on Castle, Sheik could tell that Castle was in a different mind frame and he hoped that a night out would ease Castle's mind.

After being robbed and just barely making it out alive, Castle refused to be caught slippin' again. Shit, had it not been for the bitch Parker runnin' her fuckin' mouth about his business at the salon, then he would have never been a target in the first place is how he felt. So he didn't feel at all bad about killing the bitch. And he damn sure wouldn't feel bad about killing the niggas who stripped him whenever he found their asses. So far all he had to go off of was a name: Rob. He remembered overhearing one of the jack-boys call out that name, and now he was determined to match the name with a face so they could face off. But until then, he still had an operation to run.

Sheik hit the blunt once more, then passed it to his mans and said, "Tried warnin' you that bitch Parker was no good from the start. The bitch was just too fuckin' amazed by your lifestyle."

"Tell me about it. I just thought that she would be a good asset to the operation, since I needed another trafficker," Castle replied and then puffed the weed.

"Look, good thing her ass didn't know about the main stash house 'cause then you may have been left with absolutely no paper and product. It's fucked up that your duck-off spot was hit, but the shit that was taken won't be much to get back."

"I feel you. However I ain't gonna let those niggas get away with comin' for me like that."

"You don't even know who the hell they are."

"I'll find out. What I do know is one of the niggas name is Rob, and I already have a good idea how to find out exactly who he is and how to find his ass," Castle told him.

"You know I'm down for whatever. Real shit, I want them niggas dead just as much as you do," said Sheik.

The traffic light flipped green and then the Bentley pulled off with Castle peering out of the window at the falling snow-flakes as the wintertime crept up. He thought about how he had to make up for the cash and work that he was robbed of. But overall, Castle wanted to dead the niggas who had the fuckin' audacity to rob him.

CHAPTER 3

In the front room of Shanta's place, she and Kat sat on the leather couch having glasses of wine. They each had tried getting in touch with Parker, but to no avail. After confronting Parker about Castle, they hadn't heard from her since, so they figured that her ass must not be talking to either of them still. Parker being their bestie, Shanta and Kat just wanted what was best for her, and they didn't think that was Castle. If only they knew that Castle was the worst thing to ever happen to Parker.

"I know Parker's mad at us, but her ass could still at least text back," Shanta said after checking her iPhone for the fourth time for a text from Parker. None.

"Parker's my bitch and all, but I don't care about her being big mad. She needed to hear the real from us," Kat expressed. She sipped at her glass of wine.

"Right? Even still, it's not like her to go days without talking to us no matter how mad she is."

"Unless it's that nigga, Castle, keeping her from talking to us." Kat didn't know just how true her guess was.

"Can't believe that she let Castle use her. And I'm sure his ass don't even care about what happens to her, because niggas like him puts their money over bitches. I'm afraid that something bad will happen to Parker if she doesn't leave Castle." Shanta didn't realize that it was already too late.

"Shan, I don't want anything to happen to our girl either. But if Parker wants to be with Castle, then that's on her."

"And you're right about that, Kat. I just find it strange that she isn't replying to us at all," Shan said.

"I'm sure she's okay," Kat said.

Shanta grabbed her iPhone. "I'll call her mom to see if she has heard from Parker." When Parker's mother answered the call, Shanta could hear her weeping and asked her what was wrong. Once hearing the bad news that Parker was dead, she cried out, "Oh, God, no!"

"What's the matter, Shan?" Kat wanted know.

Shanta looked to her with tormented eyes. "It's Parker. She's dead..." Her voice faded.

Kat dropped her glass of wine and gasped. "Not Parker! I can't believe she's dead!"

While on the call with Parker's mother, Shanta learned of the details leading to her death. And after learning that Parker was considered collateral damage during a robbery gone bad on Castle, it made Shan think back to the night that she and Don were victimized. Unlike herself, Parker wasn't fortunate enough to make it out with her life. Shanta couldn't help but fault Castle for the tragedy.

Shanta offered Parker's mother her condolences before ending the call. She turned to Kat and wept. "Why couldn't Parker just listen to us?"

"It's not our fault or hers, Shan," Kat said.

"The only one whose fault it is, is Castle. If it wasn't for him, then Parker would be here with us right now." Even though Shanta didn't know that Castle was the one who had actually taken Parker's life, she faulted him for it because he put Parker in harm's way.

Kat sat beside her girl on the couch and pulled Shan's head onto her chest in comfort. "We're going to miss Parker a lot. She was like our sis. And no matter what we were going through she loved us, as much as we loved her," she said in a soothing voice.

"Parker didn't deserve to lose her life. So we have to make sure her life isn't lost in vain." Shan looked into Kat's tear-filled eyes and said, "She deserves for us to make sure she's never forgotten."

The pain Shan and Kat felt behind the loss of Parker was deep.

***

"You sure this is the place?"

"Yeah, I'm sure this is it."

Rich, along with T-Mac and Danger, were at the hookah lounge. It was their third night in a row being there with expectations of running across Castle. The lounge was occupied by patrons but thus far, Castle was a no show. This was the exact lounge that Castle had met up with Don on a few occasions, and Rich was expecting to catch him there so they could talk money. Therefore, Rich just had to show up until he happened to come upon Castle, because it was his only chance at gain the plug he wanted and more so needed.

"We been here three nights in a row and still haven't seen Castle," Rich complained.

"Maybe tonight he'll show up," Danger said. He took a smoke from the hookah.

T-Mac sipped at his glass of Henny then added, "Instead of bein' here night after night lookin' for the nigga Castle, we should be out lookin' for the niggas who're tryna murk us."

"Listen, Swindle or Rob ain't hard to find. But first we need to find Castle so we can have a plug. Besides, we can't beef if our money ain't right," Rich explained. He grabbed up his glass of Remy and swirled the liquor a couple times.

"Well, whenever Castle does show up, then you shouldn't just bombard him 'cause his goons may get the wrong idea, feel me?" Danger advised.

"Yeah, I feel you. I know how I'll get his attention," Rich replied with a plan in mind. He took a swig from his glass.

After the trio had a few more drinks and smoked some hookah, the night grew later and it was beginning to seem as if Castle would be a no-show once again - that was, until Castle happened to arrive. And it seemed everyone knew he was present on the scene with the way all eyes were on him, from niggas and bitches alike. However, Rich paid the nigga no mind because he didn't know that this was none other than the drug boss, Castle.

Danger nudged Rich with an elbow and told him, "There's the nigga Castle now." He then nodded towards Castle for Rich to take a look.

Castle was dripped in ice with two Cuban link chains around his neck and a busted down AP timepiece on his wrist. Even his attire was expensive. He rocked a Givenchy sweater with the matching belt and sneakers. And the four niggas along with him, one being Sheik, were also drippy in ice and designer wear. They flanked Castle as if ready to give or take a bullet for him at will. Rich thought that Castle was nothing less than the symbol of a boss.

Making his way through the lounge, Castle took a seat on a huge black leather wraparound couch and his crew followed suit. Almost immediately there were numerous niggas and bitches alike approaching Castle, most of whom he barely spoke a word to, and his crew rushed them along. He wasn't really at the lounge for social hour. He was there to unwind. Besides, Castle didn't care to have many close to him after being robbed because he didn't know who the fuck to trust.

"That nigga must be a Trap God with how many people he has praising him," Rich guessed from his observation.

"Now I see why Don wanted to have him as the plug," T-Mac input.

"So, how do you plan to get his attention?" Danger asked.

"I got a plan in mind." Rich waved over a light-skinned, thick-ass bottle girl. "Shorty, why don't you take a bottle of Rosé Belair over to that guy who's all iced out? Tell him it's courtesy of Don." He pulled out a bankroll from the pocket of his Off White denim jeans and handed her five crisp blue strip hundreds and added, "Keep the rest as a tip."

The bottle girl went on her way to do as she was directed. She approached Castle's table with the bottle of Rosé and handed it over to him, pointing out who it was courtesy of. Castle looked puzzled. He had heard Don fucked around and gotten himself murked some time back, and Castle didn't recognize the nigga whom the bottle girl had pointed out to him. Castle spoke some words to the bottle girl, who then turned on her red bottom heels and headed back towards Rich.

"Your icy homeboy says he would like to have a talk with you," the bottle girl told him.

"Thanks, shorty." Rich smiled at her before she turned on her way. He then looked to his boys and said, "Stay here while I go and talk with Castle."

"Sure you don't want us there on security?" T-Mac asked.

"Yeah, I'm sure. I just don't want to give him the wrong impression if I'm gonna get him to talk money."

Danger leaned back in his seat. "You go ahead and talk with him, and we'll secure you from here."

Standing from the table, Rich knocked back the remains from his glass of Remy before stepping over to Castle. Instantly the goons shot to their feet while Castle and Sheik stayed seated, and Rich didn't even flinch. Observing from across the lounge, T-Mac was finna hurry over there until Danger told him to be easy. Rich and Castle held eyes and studied one another a moment.

"'Preciate the bottle," Castle said and then turned the bottle up to his lips. "Now, mind tellin' me who the fuck you really are? 'Cause you damn sure ain't Don."

"My name's Rich. And as much as I admired Don, I ain't tryna be him. But he was my brotha," Rich informed him.

Castle sat up straight and peered into Rich's face, seeing that he shared features with Don. "Let's say I do believe that you're Don's brotha. How come you're here to meet with me?"

"I want the same plug that you gave my brotha."

"And why should I plug you? Besides, I don't know if you have it in you to play the game like Don did."

Rich took it upon himself to take a seat on the couch beside Castle. "Don taught me everything I know about the game, although the difference between me and him is I know how to keep a low profile. And you should plug me 'cause I can move just as much work as Don was movin', if not more. We both stand to make money doin' business with each other," he expounded.

Doing business with Rich would be beneficial for Castle to have him take over the deal he had once had with Don. Castle figured that if Rich could move as much product as Don, then he was worth pluggin'. Not to mention Castle could use a pusher as much as Rich needed a plug, because they both stood to make riches off one another.

Castle sipped at the bottle. "A'ight. I'll plug you the same as I did Don. Just know that when it comes to doin' business with me, I expect for you to come with your paper correct. Feel me?"

"Yeah, I feel you. Then fortunately my paper good."

"Swap lines with my nigga here and I'll be in touch with you," Castle told him, then Rich and Sheik exchanged cell numbers. As Rich started to step away, Castle called out behind him and stopped him in his tracks "Rich. It's fucked up that Don's gone."

"I know. And I'ma make sure he's not forgotten," Rich assured him before turning and heading back towards his boys.

"How'd it go?" T-Mac asked as Rich approached.

"Couldn't go any better," Rich answered.

"That must mean you convinced Castle to plug you," Danger piped in.

"Yeah. Once he found out that Don was my bro, then he was willin' to plug me. Now that we have this outta the way, we can tend to other shit. Look, let's bounce." Rich turned for the exit with his boys following suit.

Meantime, Castle remained in the lounge. He sipped at the bottle of Rosé.

Sheik watched as Rich made an exit. "Castle, you think Rich will be as beneficial to us as Don was?"

"We'll see. I just hope that he don't end up goin' out like Don did," Castle replied. He understood why Rich was assuming the position his brother once held in the game, which was to keep Don's reputation alive.

Unbeknownst to Rich and Castle, they were out to dead the same nigga in Rob. Rob and his gang had taken something that meant a lot to them both, which was Rich's brother and Castle's money. And now they both wanted to get revenge.

Martell "Troublesome" Bolden

CHAPTER 4

Shanta, followed by Kat, entered the hair salon. It was the first time they were there without Parker since her death, and it felt unusual for them. However, they had to learn to live on with their own lives.

Shan and Kat each checked in with their hairstylists before taking a seat and awaiting their appointments. While finishing up a client's hair, Trina noticed Shan and Kat had entered the salon then instantly Trina felt guilt bubble up in her gut. She knew that eventually she would have to face Parker's friends. If only they knew she was two faced.

"It doesn't feel the same us being here without Parker," Kat said.

"I know, right. I'm just so used to her being with us," Shanta replied.

"I miss Parker so much."

"Me too." Shan shifted towards Kat and added, "I still can't help but feel that Castle's at fault for what happened to her."

"Once we found out what he's involved in, I knew then he was bad for her. I just wish Parker would have listened to us."

"Kat, if anybody knows exactly what happened to Parker, it's Castle," Shan suggested.

Kat looked at her with steady eyes. "You're right."

If only you bitches knew, Trina mused deviously. While the girls talked among themselves, she discreetly eavesdropped. Trina agreed that what had happened to Parker was partially Castle's fault. But of course, Trina felt a sense of guile for being the one to use Parker to set up Castle for Rob, which ultimately led to Parker's death. Although had it not been for Parker boasting about her man's business, then she wouldn't have been caught in the crossfire – at least, that's how Trina felt. And she just didn't want it to be known that she had a part in what happened to Parker. Unbeknownst to Shanta and Kat their bestie was now dead partially because of Trina, and she preferred to keep it that way.

Shanta sighed. "Parker was too good for Castle."

"Well, good girls like bad boys, and that's a fact," Kat added. "Speaking of which, what's been going on with you and what's-his-name? I noticed that you haven't been with him lately."

"His name's Rob. And I'd rather not talk about him now." Shan found it hard to talk about Rob after finding out that he had something to do with Don's murder.

"Sounds to me like whatever it is, you and him are having trouble."

"It's more troubling than you'll believe. Rob is a good nigga, but he's bad for me," Shanta admitted.

"And what is it that makes him so bad for you, Shan?" Kat inquired curiously.

"Girl, it's——" She started to tell Kat the truth about Rob, but then decided against it. "It's not something I want to talk about now."

Kat placed a hand on Shan's arm and said, "Well, whenever you're ready to talk about it then I'm here for you."

"Thanks, girl."

Trina couldn't believe what she had heard while eavesdropping on the girls. She was upset to learn that Shanta was with Rob. Even though Trina and Rob weren't officially together, she still was possessive of him. And it hurt her that Rob was with Shan but didn't want to be in a committed relationship with after all she had done for him. She was his down bitch and should be his only bitch is how Trina felt. Seething, she mused, *This bitch best leave my man alone.*

***

Trina drove home with a lot on her mind after work. She stepped into her apartment, finding Rob seated on the couch watching *Power* on the flat screen TV and smoking a blunt of exotic weed. He was still laying low at her place while he healed up. Once Trina slammed the door shut with a thud, then Rob could read that she had an attitude about something. Trina set her Gucci handbag on the end table and took a seat on the couch without offering Rob a kiss or even a word.

"I guess your ass is mad about some shit," Rob pointed out and then pulled on the blunt of za. "Look, I—"

"Shanta?" Trina hurled out, cutting his words short. She eyed him through slits and folded her arms across her chest.

Rob was caught off guard in the moment and he didn't know how to respond. He glanced over at Trina and responded, "What about Shanta?"

"Shanta's one of my clients, and apparently she's one of your bitches. I overheard her mention how you and her are having trouble. Rob, I don't know how long you been fuckin' with the bitch, but it's not good for you."

"Listen, Trina, don't try to tell me what's good for me or not. You don't know shit!" he raved.

"And do you know that the bitch, Parker, who I used to set up Castle was Shanta's friend? So, if she finds out you had anything to do with what happened to Parker, then it could be big trouble for you, Rob!" she griped.

Now Rob remembered why he had thought the bitch who Castle had scooped up from the salon had looked so familiar: because he had seen her with Shanta before. He couldn't imagine how Shanta must feel after losing her friend. He hated to admit that Trina was right. If Shan found out he had something to do with what happened to Parker, then it would be too much for her to handle, especially after her finding out that he had something to do with what happened to Don. Rob hoped to mend things with Shan, and he didn't care how Trina felt about them being together.

Rob muted the volume on the TV. "Look, Shanta won't find out a damn thing. So you don't have to worry about me and her. A'ight?" he said sternly.

Trina shifted towards him in her seat. "Rob, so you want to be with her over me after all the shit I've done for you? Do you love the bitch?"

"Listen," he began calmly, "just keep playin' your position, will you? And so, you know, love don't mean shit if it's not between the right nigga and bitch."

Pulling Trina close to him, Rob pecked her forehead. She didn't quite know how to feel about him in that moment. As Trina headed for the adjacent bathroom to take a shower, Rob called after her, stopping her in her tracks.

"Just know that you're right for me, but I'm bad for you," he told her.

Trina eyed him through slits and said, "Bad boys ain't no good." She turned on her way.

Rob set back in his seat and puffed on the blunt. He had to admit that Trina was right about the fact that if Shanta was to find out about him having a part in what happened to Parker, then it could cause him more trouble. He already had to figure out how to make amends with Shanta, and he had an idea of how he would do so. But first things first: he had to get even with Bone. Until Rob was healed up he would lay low, which was probably best since Rich was still looking for him. And unbeknownst to him, Castle also wanted his head. Rob couldn't help but feel like he was against all odds.

***

The Mayfair mall was busy with shoppers. Shanta and Kat had stopped there after leaving the salon. They were doing some shopping in order to make themselves feel better and take their minds off of things. While taking a break from their shopping spree, the girls sat at a table in the mall's food court, having themselves a bite to eat. Kat noticed that Shan didn't seem herself at all today. Normally while they shopped, Shan would criticize her excessive spending habits, but today she just let Kat splurge. Knowing her girl all too well, Kat knew that something was troubling Shanta.

"Bitch, what's troubling you?" Kat wanted to know.

Shanta sighed and said, "It's nothing."

"Shan, I know you better than anyone. I can tell that it's something. Is it Parker?"

"No. I miss our girl, but it's not Parker."

"Then it must be Rob. Because lately you barely speak a word about him," Kat pointed out.

"Just let it go, Kat."

"Unh-unh, I won't just let it go. If he did something to hurt you, then let me know because I ain't letting no nigga hurt my sis and get away with it. That's on period. So, what did his ass do, Shan?"

Shanta was hurting more than she let on. She didn't ex-actly know how to come out and tell Kat that all the while she thought Rob was really a good nigga, he turned out to be worse than she could imagine. It wasn't that she thought Kat would judge her. Shan was just embarrassed at the fact that she didn't realize who Rob truly was until it was too late.

Once Kat noticed the tears sail down her friend's cheeks, then she knew it was something bad troubling Shan concern-ing Rob. She moved over to the chair beside Shan and com-forted her. "Girl, whatever it is, you can tell me, sis. I'm here for you."

"There's no easy way to tell you this, but the reason I haven't been with Rob lately is because he had something to do with what happened to Don," Shan told her.

"Are you sure?"

Shan nodded. "After Rich happened to see me with him, then Rich told me who Rob really is. At first I couldn't believe it, but when I confronted Rob, then he admitted to it with the hopes that I would forgive him."

"Shan, I can't even imagine how you must feel knowing that Rob had something to do with killing Don. Not to mention the loss of your unborn child. How do you think Rob feels about it?"

"I don't even care how Rob feels. And I wish that I never met him," Shan sobbed.

Kat pressed Shan's head against her chest as Shan cried her eyes out. "Good thing you found out who Rob really is sooner rather than later. Now you can move on from his ass."

"I just feel like I betrayed Don by getting with someone who had something to do with what happened to him. I don't think I can forgive myself."

"Shan, don't blame yourself, because you didn't know who Rob was when you met him. And you never did anything to betray Don, so don't even think like that. Listen, Don knew you were devoted to him and that's why he loved you. Don't ever forget that."

"I won't. Thank you for being here for me," Shanta said earnestly.

"Always, girl. Now, let's get you home. We've done enough shopping for one day." Kat knew that Shanta needed her, and as her bestie, she would be there to console Shan. She was sure Shanta was heartbroken that Rob was the one who killed Don, because it was obvious that both men had a place in her heart.

CHAPTER 5

Out of habit, Bone perpetually checked his rearview mirror for any signs of Twelve or opps. With snow falling like a thin veil from the night sky it made it difficult to drive on the wet streets in case he needed to put the pedal to the metal in order to make a clean getaway for any reason. Arriving at his destination, Bone pulled his Yukon into the lot of a local gas station and then parked beside the Chrysler that belonged to Swindle.

It had been a week since they had last seen one another and Bone was there meeting with Swindle in order to collect the paper owed to him for the bricks he fronted from the lick on Castle. Bone expected Swindle to have all of his paper, and if not, then Swindle should expect for Bone to burn him.

Bone strapped his Mac-10 around his neck before stepping outta his Yukon, then he stepped into the passenger seat of the Chrysler with the weapon on full display. Swindle wasn't even bothered in the least bit by the weapon being on display because he had his Glock with a thirty-shot clip laying in his lap with a hand resting on its butt. It was nothing personal for either of them. It was just business. And they understood that in the streets, business is cold but fair.

Swindle reached into the glove compartment and grabbed the brown paper bag, then handed it over to Bone. "Inside is the fifty bands. Plus ten more just for good business."

"It's always good doin' business with you," Bone responded as he took a look at the cash inside the bag.

"Same. But we still have some unfinished business to conduct."

Bone looked over to him. "And what's that?"

"It's Rich. Now that Rob is dead, we don't have to worry about him coming for us, but Rich won't stop until he either gets revenge for what we did to his brotha or he dies tryin'."

"Then we'll make sure his ass dies. Soon as you get the drop on Rich, let me know and we'll slide on him."

"I got Vito and some shooters out lookin' for him as we speak. But that nigga ain't gonna be easy to slide on 'cause he knows how to move in these streets. So we gotta be a step ahead of him, or he'll fuck around, get a heads up on us, then it could be curtains. And I'ont know about you, but with all this fuckin' money I'm havin', I ain't ready to be buried in a grave," Swindle told him in all seriousness.

"No doubt," Bone agreed. "We'll put that nigga in a grave before he sees it comin'."

"I'm with that. Be in touch."

Bone dapped up Swindle before stepping outta the whip into the snowfall with the brown paper bag in hand and the Mac-10 dangling from around his neck. He stepped into his Yukon then pulled out of the gas station lot into traffic while beatin' Lil Poppa's tune "RIP".

Thinking back on what Swindle had said, neither did Bone want to meet an early grave. He also wanted to enjoy the money he had. And he couldn't help but think of the money that Rob had mentioned having buried away. Even though he had come up on close to six hundred Gs from the lick on Castle after betraying his comrades, Bone refused to let the money in the grave go unclaimed. And it was all his to claim now that Rob was dead and gone. Or so he thought.

***

Pulling the Porsche truck into the strip mall parking lot, T-Mac parked beside the Bentley truck as Rich had instructed. Rich was there to meet up with Castle. After the two had met at the hookah lounge a week prior, Rich had gotten in touch with Castle in order to cop some weight, and this was the location that Castle had picked to meet up with Rich to do business. He preferred to meet in public places in case a nigga had the idea to jack him, especially after what had gone down with Rob. And Rich just wanted to take care of business so he could get back to the money.

Reaching into the backseat, Rich grabbed the Prada backpack filled with cash out of Danger's lap. He then stuffed the .45 Glock on his waist before stepping out of the Porsche, leaving T-Mac and Danger in the whip while he went to make the deal. Once Rich entered the rear seat of the Bentley, he was seated beside Castle. Sheik set in the front passenger seat with a MK-18 assault rifle across his lap, and a goon acted as their chauffeur. Rich and Castle each proceeded with caution of one another. It was nothing personal, just business.

"Here's the seventy-five Gs," Rich said as he showed Castle the cash. "Now, where's the three bricks?"

"Sheik, give him what he came for," Castle instructed.

Sheik came from under his seat with three individually packaged kilos and then handed them back to Rich.

While examining the keys, Rich noticed the familiar Libra logo stamped on each of them. He dumped the stacks of cash from the Prada backpack into Castle's lap then replaced the keys inside of it. "Don't you wanna count up the paper?"

"Already told you that when it comes to doin' business with me, I expect for you to come with your paper correct. So I shouldn't have to count it up."

"And I already told you that my paper good."

"Then we're good for business," Castle said.

"Good." Rich was finna get out of the truck when Castle halted him.

"Make sure you watch out for jack-boys in the streets, 'cause they're always out lurkin' on us dope-boys," Castle warned.

Rich lifted his shirt just enough to display the butt of his Glock with its extended clip protruding and told him, "Jack-boys best watch out for me. Especially the one who murked Don. And whenever I catch that nigga, Rob, then his ass is dead."

As soon as the name Rob was mentioned, then Castle looked to Sheik, bewildered. Castle couldn't believe that, of all niggas, Rob was also the one who had poked Don. He figured that Rich wanted Rob dead just as bad as he did.

Castle shifted towards Rich and said, "Look, if you know where to find this Rob nigga, then let me know, and I'll send some shooters at his ass. 'Cause believe it or not, him and his boys poked me too. Shit, I'm lucky to be alive."

"And how can you be so sure that it was Rob who stripped you?"

"I couldn't get a look at the nigga 'cause he was masked up, but I heard one of his boys say Rob's name while they had guns pointed in my fuckin' face," Castle replied heatedly. He planted a hand on Rich's shoulder and looked him in the eyes. "Rich, I understand that Rob took your brotha's life, and I want his ass dead just as bad as you do 'cause he was finna take mine too."

Rich could see in Castle's eyes that he was serious. "Right now, I'ont know where to find Rob, but if I figure it out, then I'll let you know. However, I'd rather be the one to personally smoke his ass."

"And I'd just rather him than me."

"Fa sho'," Rich concurred. "I'll be in touch."

Once Rich stepped out of the Bentley, then Castle n'em pulled off. Both of them were surprised to know that Rob had been the one to cause them each a major loss in the game. They had to do something to get even.

"How'd it go?" Danger asked as Rich stepped back into the passenger seat of the Porsche.

"Y'all ain't gon' believe this shit," Rich breathed and handed the backpack containing the birds back to Danger.

T-Mac push-started the whip. "What shit?"

"The shit that went down with Castle. He also got robbed by the nigga, Rob."

"So Rob just goin' around layin' niggas down like it ain't shit," Danger said bitterly.

"Apparently. Castle told me that while bein' stripped, he overheard one of the jack-boys say Rob's name. And now he wants the nigga's head too. But not if I put a bullet in his head first," Rich told them.

"No cap," T-Mac responded as he pulled out of the parking lot.

Danger rested a hand on the Draco in his lap. "That nigga, Rob, gotta pay in blood for what he did to Don. And we can't forget about Swindle."

"Fa sho'. We gon' spill both of them bitch-ass niggas' blood on the strength of Don," Rich assured.

"And let's not forget about C-note," Danger added.

"Until then, we'll keep our minds on the money and our fingers on the trigga. And now that we're plugged with Castle, it won't be nothin' for us to get our money and weight up."

Now that Rich had plugged in with Castle they were bound to make one another lots of money. And money might be their motive, but Rob had given them both a motive to kill.

***

In the front room of her apartment, Kayla set on the leather couch, drowning her sorrows in a bottle of Remy with thoughts of TJ on her mind. Ever since she had learned about TJ's death, she hadn't left her place while in mourning. What hurt her most was the fact that she knew TJ had planned to leave the stick-up game in order to live a normal life with her. But sadly he was killed during what was to be his final lick. Kayla didn't know what she would do without TJ because he was the one for her. Now she felt all alone and just needed someone to be there for her.

Kayla couldn't help but reminisce about all of the memorable moments she had shared with TJ. She had no intentions to fall for him since she was with Bone at the time. But after confiding in TJ while Bone was on lockdown, she had unexpectedly gained feelings for TJ and obviously the feeling was mutual. Although there were times when she wondered how things would be had she stayed with Bone. However, she had chosen to be with TJ and was genuinely happy with her choice. Tears began to sail down Kayla's cheeks as she reminisced.

Needing to clear her head, Kayla decided that she would take herself a bath. She made her way into the bathroom and ran a hot bath, then gathered all of her bathing essentials. After undressing she stepped into the bathtub and submerged in the hot bubble bath allowing herself to soak. While she tried to gather a peace of mind, there came a disturbing knock on the front door.

Who the hell could that be disturbing my peace? Kayla frustratedly contemplated. She wasn't expecting any company, and quite frankly, she didn't care for any. After climbing out the tub she wrapped herself in a huge towel and then padded through the front room barefoot to shoo away whoever was at the door. Upon pulling open the door, she was surprised to see who was standing on the doorstep.

"Bone?" Kayla uttered. He made his way inside past her without a word. "Hell are you doing here?" she inquired as he shut the door behind him.

"Thought you could use someone to lean on in this hard time," Bone replied, and she didn't object. Looking around the apartment, he noticed it was unkempt. He saw the half-drunk bottle of liquor on the coffee table. Kayla looked as though she had been crying her eyes out. He could tell she was struggling with the loss of TJ. "Fucked up what happened to TJ."

"I still can't believe he's gone. I feel all alone." She grew teary-eyed.

Bone stepped closer to her and said, "I'm here for you, Kay."

"I appreciate it. But I still haven't even heard from Rob."

And you won't, Bone said to himself introspectively. "Look, Rob didn't make it out either. None of the others did."

"So how did you?" Kayla wanted to know.

"If it wasn't for TJ takin' a bullet for me, then I may not be here right now." Quiet as kept, he had also plotted to murk TJ along with the others. Bone pulled out a bankroll from the pocket of his Blue Bands Only loose fit denim jeans, then set it atop the coffee table and said, "I know money can't buy happiness, but that's ten Gs on the strength of TJ. I'm sure losin' him is hard on you."

"Harder than you'll ever know. Especially since he told me that lick would be his final one. Now I just can't stop thinking about the future TJ and I was supposed to share."

"Yeah, I know the feelin' all too well," he replied in a lowered voice.

Kayla stood with her arms folded beneath her breasts and her weight shifted to one side. "Apparently you mean the future you and I were supposed to share. Bone, I thought about it at times, but what's the use since I chose to be with TJ. And it was never about him being better than you in any way. It was merely about him being there for me when I needed someone most."

"Well, I'm here for you now. And it seems like you need someone."

"Bone, I do need someone right now but..." Her words faded when he wiped away the tears on her cheeks.

Bone grabbed her on either side of her small waist and pulled her close for a kiss. Kayla didn't resist. She went along with it, wrapping her arms around the nape of his neck and kissed his lips. In that moment, she forgot about her future with TJ and remembered what she had had with Bone in the past. Her mind was telling her no, but her body was telling her otherwise.

They kissed passionately as their hands explored one another's frame. Kayla's pussy was wet and Bone's dick was hard. He lifted her off her feet by her ass and she wrapped her legs around his torso as he carried her into the bedroom. Bone lay her back on the king-sized bed, then removed the towel from covering her and exposed her brown skin. Kayla prudently removed the gun from his waist and set it on the nightstand then began helping him out of his attire.

"Wait, Bone," Kayla spoke up and stopped him. She grabbed the towel from the floor and rewrapped herself. "This is just morally wrong and TJ damn sure wouldn't approve of us sleeping together. I know I need someone here for me right now, but not like this."

Bone scoffed. "And where the fuck was your moral compass when you slept with TJ, huh?"

"Are you serious? You're going to come at me like that? Bone, you should just leave."

"Kay, don't let your morals stop you now," he told her as he tried forcing himself on her.

Kayla pushed him away and shouted, "Leave…now!"

Bone grabbed up his gun and glared at her. "A'ight. I'll leave." He replaced the gun on his waist and said, "If you change your mind, then just hit my line. You'll need me before I need you." Then he turned and made his way out of the apartment, leaving Kayla to her thoughts.

Kayla hurried to the front door and locked it behind him. She slid back down against the door, not knowing exactly what to think of Bone in that moment. Unbeknownst to her, Bone had only came over with ill intentions to fuck her just to get even now that TJ was dead and gone. As Kayla thought about not having TJ there to protect her from Bone tears wet her cheeks. Looking over at the bankroll that Bone had left atop the coffee table for her on the strength of TJ, she knew it was blood money. If only she knew that Bone had spilled the blood of TJ and the others for it.

Kayla buried her face in her palms and bawled as she contemplated, *No amount of money is worth losing TJ.*

CHAPTER 6

It was yet another day at the hair salon for Trina. And as usual, she overheard bitches gossiping and bragging about their niggas. She didn't understand why bitches were comfortable enough to tell all of their niggas' business. But it wasn't for her to tell them otherwise is how she felt. Besides, Trina found the info useful for a potential lick to put Rob on.

The Bentley truck slid to the curb before the salon then out came Castle. He remembered right before smokin' Parker she had informed him that the only person she told anything about him was her hairstylist, Trina. Therefore, Castle was convinced that she was the one who had lined him up to be laid down by Rob, so he took it upon himself to show up at the salon to confront the conniving bitch.

While Trina was busy doing a client's hair, Castle entered the salon, followed closely behind by Sheik. All of the girls' chatter subsided as their admiring eyes were on the two niggas drippin' in jewels and designer clothes, including Trina. Having never seen Castle herself before, Trina was sleeping on who he was, but she was in for a rude awakening.

"Which one of you bitches in here is Trina?" Castle demanded, glaring from one hairstylist to the next.

"I-I am," Trina admitted reluctantly after everyone cut their eyes at her. "Um, do we know each other?"

Castle stepped up on her and sniped, "Nah. But we knew the same person. Parker."

Who the hell is he to her? Trina contemplated in confusion. "Yeah, I'm Parker's hairstylist. And you are?"

"I'm sure she told you all about me. The name's Castle." He stared her dead in the face to measure her reaction.

"Look, I don't know what you want, but whatever it is with Parker has nothing to do with me." She didn't want to let him see her sweat.

"Wrong. It has everything to do with you. 'Cause I'm sure you used Parker to line me up to be robbed. And now she's gone and so is my fuckin' money," he snarled.

Trina's nerves were beginning to get the better of her. "Y-you have the wrong person," she replied quickly in a quivering voice.

"You're right about that. The person I'm really lookin' for is Rob. And all you have to do is tell me where I can find his ass."

"I d-don't know," she lied through her teeth.

Growing impatient, Castle pulled the Glock from his waist and held it dangling at his side. "Bitch, don't fuckin' lie to me. Now tell me where the hell his ass at!"

"I already told you that I don't know!"

"Since you won't tell me where Rob is, then you can die for him." Castle trained the barrel on her dome…

Sheik used a hand to lower the gun, stopping Castle from pulling the trigger and sparing Trina. "Now isn't the time or place."

"Listen up, bitch, tell Rob's ass to give my money back and it might be worth him keepin' his life," Castle told her briskly. He turned and headed out of the salon with Sheik in tow, leaving everyone in the salon in silence.

Trina sighed a breath of relief that her life had been spared. She had almost lost her life trying to protect Rob, and she did-n't even know if he would do the same for her. Never did Trina expect for Castle to come for her, and now she realized that she was as much at fault for both him being stripped and Par-ker being murked by Rob.

"Why'd you stop me from smokin' that lyin'-ass bitch?" Castle wanted to know as one of his goons pulled the Bentley away from the curb outside of the salon while he and Sheik rode in back. He was heated about Sheik sparing the bitch Trina, worthless life. "That bitch knows where Rob is."

"Which is one reason why I stopped you from smokin' her," Sheik told him. "Besides, there were too many damn witnesses to smoke her right then."

"You right. And it's not even her who I want. It's Rob."

"She's gonna lead us to him, li'l do she know. After the situation back at the salon, she'll run to tell Rob all about it. And we'll tail her to where his ass is hidin' out."

"Good idea. And when we do find him, first I want you to get that nigga to pay me my cash back before you dead his ass. 'Cause a dead man can't pay. Got me?" Castle laid out.

"Yeah, I got you. But if he try me, then I'ma leave his ass dead, cash or not," Sheik forewarned him.

***

Without any words, Trina grabbed up her handbag and hurried out of the salon for her Kia parked out front. She peeled off down the street, speeding on the way to her place. Not checking her surroundings, she never noticed the Bentley truck a few vehicles back tailing her the entire time. As expected, Trina was on her way to warn Rob that Castle was looking for him.

Arriving at her place, Trina parked, jumped out of the car, and then hurried into the apartment complex.

Rob was finna step out of the apartment to go grab a bite to eat when Trina came rushing inside. He could read the franticness etched on her face and knew something was the matter.

"Rob, he showed up at the salon looking for you!" Trina cried out.

"Who?" Rob wanted to know.

"Castle, that's who."

Rob figured Castle knew of him because his name had been called out during the lick, which is why he now regretted not taking out Castle then. "I know how Castle knows of me, but, how the hell would he know who you are?"

"Parker must've told him about me. He was going to kill me if I didn't tell him where to find you."

He gripped her arm. "And what did you tell him, Trina?"

"Told him that I didn't know where you were, alright? Now please let go of my arm, you're hurting me," Trina whimpered.

"My bad. I didn't mean to hurt you." Rob released his grip.

"Only reason he didn't kill my ass right then is because the guy who was with him spared me. Rob, I'm so scared that if Castle find out you're hiding out at my place then he'll kill us both." Tears slid down her cheeks.

Rob thumbed away her tears. "Don't be scared 'cause I'll find Castle first and deal with his ass," he told her.

"He wanted me to tell you that if you give him the money back, then he'll let you live," she reported.

"I'ont believe that Castle will let me live whether I give him back the money or not."

"Rob, please just give it back to him," Trina begged.

"Don't you understand, Trina? A kingpin like Castle would never let a jack-boy get away with takin' his hard-earned money. Only way to make shit even is if I kill him or he kills me. And I'd rather him than me. So if you ain't with me, then you're against me," Rob stated.

Trina folded her arms beneath her breasts and displayed attitude. "If I wasn't with you, then I would've just told Castle where you are when he threatened my life, Rob."

"Listen," Rob pulled her close to him by the waist, "all we have to do is play it safe for now. Best way to do that is by you actin' normal and me watchin' my back. We won't have to worry about Castle after I murk that nigga."

"O-okay. I'll do whatever it is you need me to do," Trina replied.

"Then why don't you start by goin' to grab somethin' to eat," Rob directed her. He kissed her lips. "I'll be here when you get back."

Once Trina left out of the apartment, Rob looked outside from behind the window blind. He observed Trina as she stepped into her whip and then drove on her way to grab a bite to eat as directed. There was no vehicle tailing her and none parked on the street that seemed out of place, so Rob figured he was in the clear of anyone knowing where he was laying his head. However, Rob realized that he shouldn't stay there for much longer because it was only a matter of time until someone found out where he was. Unbeknownst to Rob, Trina had already unknowingly led Castle to him.

If Castle thinks I'm foolish enough to believe that he and I will be even after I give him the money back, then he must be the fool, Rob contemplated. He knew that the only way for him and Castle to get even was by killing one another. Besides, Rob didn't even have the money that belonged to Castle. However, Rob planned to take it back from Bone by any means.

***

While eating their meals at the barbecue joint, Rich and T-Mac occupied a booth. With all the beef going on in the streets lately, they barely had any time to sit and talk over a meal. Not to mention that now that they were plugged with Castle they were busy flippin' the product. However, Rich just wanted to be sure that they didn't let the beef get in the way of them gettin' to the bag.

Kat entered the eatery. She was there to pick up the order of food she had called in earlier. Once noticing Rich sitting in the booth, she made her way over to him. "Hey, Rich," Kat greeted as she stepped up. She offered T-Mac a wave, who returned her a head nod.

"'Sup," Rich replied. There was something about Kat that he didn't take to.

"Look, Shanta told me about the shit with Rob and it's fucked up. I know you're still affected by what happened to Don just as much as Shan is, but don't let it get the best of you."

Rich studied her a moment. "Kat, I 'preciate your attempt to console a nigga, but I can do without it. And I'll make sure me and Shan get some vindication when it comes to the nigga Rob, and what he did to my brotha. Trust, it hasn't gotten the best of me. It just brought out the worst in me."

She indicated his sharp tone. "I didn't mean to rub you wrong. I just wanted to offer my support."

"Well, that's what I got Brittany for."

Kat smacked her full lips. "Please, that bitch ain't got shit on me. She may be a good bitch, but what you need is a bad bitch."

Rich scoffed. "Kat, I ain't gon' keep lettin' you disrespect Brittany like that. So watch your fuckin' mouth. And you ain't shit to me, so you'll never be a bitch that I want or need."

"Yo, Rich," T-Mac intervened, "take it easy, cuz. I'm sure Kat didn't mean to disrespect your girl. Why don't we just finish our meals and let shorty go about her business?" He thought Rich was being a little too hard on Kat.

Rich pushed his plate away and said, "Suddenly I lost my appetite. Let's bounce." He stood and made his way towards the exit.

"Thanks for speaking up for me," Kat said humbly.

"I got you, boo." T-Mac stood in close proximity of Kat, towering over her. He had to admit that he thought shorty was bad. "Just know that you owe me one," he told her, wearing a smirk. He then also headed for the exit.

Kat was left standing there. She didn't mean to upset Rich and she didn't realize how much he was obviously into Brittany. Maybe she didn't stand a chance with Rich, but she did appreciate how T-Mac stood up for her. All Kat wanted was a nigga who would be there for her. But she understood that everything that glitters isn't gold.

As Rich and T-Mac slid through traffic, Rich rode shotgun in silence while T-Mac pushed his Porsche truck with the music beatin'. Neither wore a seatbelt, but each had a gun in their lap just to be on the safe side. They were on the way to their trap spot in the hood as snow came down in a thin veil.

T-Mac lowered the volume on the stereo and asked, "What was that all about with Kat back at the BBQ joint?"

"Her ass just needed to know her place is all," Rich answered simply.

"Don't you think you were a li'l hard on her?"

"Look, I was just standin' up for Britt. Which is what you did for Kat back there. You feelin' her or some shit?" Rich peered at him with a quirked brow.

"Kat's a cool bitch, that's all," T-Mac responded, purposely keeping his eyes straight ahead on traffic. He thought his eyes might give away how he saw Kat. "What's more important is how you're feelin' about Brittany. And it's apparent that you feel strongly about her."

Rich leaned back in his seat. "Cuz, I'd be flodgin' if I told you that my feelin's ain't strong for her. It's just hard for a nigga to show any feelin's with how the streets got me feelin' numb."

"Then maybe you should grab Brittany and take a break from the streets. You and her go someplace nice for a change," T-Mac suggested.

"And what about you, T-Mac? With all the beef goin' on in these streets, I wouldn't wanna leave you alone."

T-Mac braked the whip at a stoplight then patted his Tec-9 and stated, "Nigga, this mu'fuckin Tec ain't for show. No cap. Besides, I'll have Danger here to watch my back. What's the worst that could go wrong in a few days?"

"A'ight," Rich agreed reluctantly. He had to admit that taking a break from the streets would be good for him. Especially taking Brittany with him because it would give him the much-needed time to enjoy her company. Rich just worried that with all the beef in the streets shit would pop off while he was absent. He looked to T-Mac and told him: "Just make sure if worse turn to worse then you'll call me."

"Will do. You just make sure to get Brittany's nails done before the trip," T-Mac said.

"Why's that?"

"'Cause she's gonna post the ring on the 'Gram after you propose," he half-joked and caused them both to share a laugh.

"Unlike you, I ain't tryna be married to the streets," Rich replied.

T-Mac smirked. "Til death do us part."

Once the red light flipped green, T-Mac pulled off with traffic and Rich turned up the volume on Peezy's tune "Good & Bad".

CHAPTER 7

Rich and Brittany were sitting out on the balcony of their Hilton hotel suite under the early morning Los Angeles sun. They were comfortably covered in plush robes while enjoying breakfast and mimosas that were delivered to their suite via room service. After their flight had landed in LAX late last night they had checked into the hotel, showered, and then fallen asleep.

Rich had decided to bring Britt along on a vacay to California and was looking forward to them spending more time together. Lately with all of the shit he had to tend to in the streets, Rich hardly had time to himself, and Brittany knew he needed a break from his street affairs. So while in Cali, Rich planned to forget about the streets back home and remember why he was with Brittany on vacay. The weather was most definitely better there than it was back home so it was easy to forget the cold streets of Milwaukee while in sunny L.A.

"Bae, I hope you enjoyin' yourself," Rich said.

"I am." Brittany sipped at her mimosa.

"Britt, I know that I haven't spent much time with you as of lately with all the shit I've been tendin' to in the streets. So I'm glad that I brought you out here with me to Cali."

"And I'm glad I'm here with you, too. But Rich, I believe you needed this time away from the streets more than I needed some time with you. Because lately you been putting a lot of your time and efforts into the streets since Don died. And I just don't want you to end up dying the same."

Rich rose to his feet and stepped over to the rail of the balcony where he got a view of the sunny L.A. scenery, with its beautiful trees and clear blue skies. He knew that Britt was right, but he couldn't just let Don's name die in the streets. So he was willing to die himself if that was what it would take to keep his brother's name alive. He believed that avenging his brother was the best way for him to honor Don's name.

"Listen, I'll admit that what happened to my brotha has motivated me to go hard in the streets. But you're right, I'ont wanna end up dead also. I'm just not afraid to," Rich expounded.

"Rich," Brittany said gingerly as she stood and then stepped up beside him. "I can see that you're still hurt behind the death of your brother. And you may not be afraid of dying, but what about me and your mom? I'm sure she fears for your life as much as I do," she expressed.

"Look, you and my mom mean a lot to me. And I'ont want either of you to live in fear of my life. But that is just the way it is."

"No, Rich. It's more to life than that. But you have to want more." A single tear slowly slid down her cheek.

Rich turned towards her and said, "You're right." He used his thumb to wipe away the tear. "I know that I'ont tell you this enough, but I love you, Brittany."

"Rich, I love you more."

In that moment Rich grabbed Brittany at the curvy hips and pulled her close, then they kissed passionately. Their tongues entangled while he grasped her ass in both hands and she coiled her arms around the nape of his neck. It was as if no one else existed while Rich and Britt were loss in the arms of each other. His dick was throbbing hard and her pussy was soaking wet.

They helped one another out of their robes and were standing on the balcony in the nude with the sun kissing their brown skin. Rich sucked on one of Britt's succulent titties while he slowly slipped two of his fingers back and forth in her wet-ass pussy. While kissing Rich on the lips and neck, Brittany guided him backwards over to the lounge chair, where she pushed him down onto it. She then fell onto her knees and grabbed his long, thick dick in both of her petite, manicured hands, then began licking and sucking on its tip all while gazing up into his lustful eyes. Her warm tongue and soft lips felt so damn good on his dick.

"Shit, baby, you suckin' me like a porn star!" Rich groaned as she sucked his dick from its base to its tip without gagging. He enjoyed the sounds her mouth made on his hardness as she slurped and spit on it. He leaned back in the chair with his eyes closed tight and his toes curled while she flicked her tongue rapidly over the tip of his dick and jacked it off. His ass cheeks clenched as he felt himself about to bust a nut. "Oh, shit! Baby, don't spit it out." He watched with bliss as Brittany cleaned off his dick with her mouth. "Now c'mere."

Rich pulled Britt atop him as he lay all the way back on the lounge chair. She straddled his face with each of her feet on either side of the floor and lowered her pussy down onto his mouth. He held her at the hips while his tongue teased her pussy lips. The scent of her Chanel fragrance made her pussy taste better, he thought. Brittany arched her back and rode his face while he used his fingers to spread her pussy lips as he rapidly flicked his tongue over her clit.

"Ooohhh, baaabe! Eat me just like that!" Brittany moaned in pleasure. She bit down on her lower lip and caressed her nipples while Rich sucked and licked on her wet-wet. Her knees clamped around his head and she began to quiver as an ocean of orgasm came over her. While finger fuckin' her, Rich darted his tongue in and out of her slit tasting her juices as she creamed in his mouth. Britt then climbed down and sat on his hard dick allowing it to fill her pussy and she began riding him like a stallion.

"Ride dis big-ass dick, boo. Ride it," Rich encouraged her as she bucked up and down on his lap. He grasped her soft ass cheeks while slamming her down on his dick and she moaned as he hit her G-spot. Brittany clenched her teeth as she felt herself about to cum again.

"Daaamn, Rich... Dis dick feels so damn good, boy!" Britt moaned. She came so much her juices were like a flowing river.

Rich stood while holding her up by her ass and Brittany held onto his shoulders and wrapped her legs around his waist. He carried her over to the balcony's rail, where he pressed her back against it, and then she reached down and grabbed his throbbing dick and replaced it inside of her slippery pussy. While drilling his hardness inside of her wetness, Britt dug her manicured nails into the flesh of Rich's back as she took the dick. And with each thrust, Rich felt like the pussy had gotten better and wetter. She gently bit on his lower lip and he fucked her harder. The pussy was so good he could no longer resist bustin' a nut.

"Oh shit, boo! Dis pussy got a nigga ready!" Rich grunted. He then came stronger than ever, feeling himself get weak in the knees. No longer having much strength, Rich planted Brittany down on her feet. He kissed her lips then said, "A nigga love your ass."

Brittany draped her arms over his shoulders. "And I love you more than you know."

The couple stood ass naked on the balcony, peering out at the L.A. skyline, while Rich stood behind Brittany, holding her in his arms. They noticed there was an elderly Black couple across from them that was out on the balcony of their own suite who had thoroughly enjoyed the sex scene. The elderly couple smiled at them and waved, and Rich and Brittany just laughed as they headed inside of their suite.

After their sex on the balcony, Rich and Brittany showered and dressed then went on with their day. Rich had a special day planned for him and Britt all the way into the night. First they started with getting a couple's massage in the hotel's spa, followed by going on a shopping spree out in Beverly Hills on Rodeo Drive, and then ending the night at one of Los Angeles' most prominent restaurants, Mr. Chow.

The couple were awaiting valet for their rental car outside of Mr. Chow following their candlelit dinner. Rich and Brittany stood arm in arm, both looking as if they were some of the rich and famous. Rich was drippin' in a cream colored Chanel polo shirt, red Off White jeans, and a Chanel belt and loafers. His man bun was in designer braids and he rocked diamond boogers in his ears, a gold Cuban link necklace, and a plain gold Cartier timepiece. And Brittany was slaying in a red body-hugging, thigh-high Chanel dress with spaghetti straps, cream colored Chanel red bottom stilettos and matching clutch purse. Her hair was wrapped and she wore minimal makeup with diamond hoop earrings and a diamond tennis bracelet. The couple looked good together.

"Dinner was nice," Brittany commented.

"Yeah, it was. But you coulda shared some of your dessert with me," Rich half-joked.

"You can get some dessert later." She smirked seductively.

"Didn't you get enough earlier, boo?"

"It's never too much."

He pulled her close. "Listen, I thought about what you said earlier. I do want more in life. And what I want most in life is you."

"Then show me how much you want me in your life, Rich. Put me before your street life."

Valet pulled up in the silver drop-top Ferrari F430 Spider. Rich opened the passenger door and helped Brittany inside, then he tipped valet before hopping over the car door into the driver seat. He then zipped off down the street in the 'Rari with its roof absent in the night L.A. traffic. As they cruised through the city of angels, the wind breathed on their faces. He shifted the 'Rari through traffic and she took in the night-lights of the city. Rich had one last spot that he wanted to bring Brittany before returning to the hotel for the night. He wanted to give her night to remember.

Arriving at one of L.A.'s beaches, Rich parked the 'Rari near the sand with a view of the Pacific Ocean spreading before them. The moon and the stars glistened on the body of water. Britt enjoyed the view. Summer Walker crooned about love through the car's speakers at a lowered volume while the couple set quietly a moment.

"Listen, Brittany," Rich began coolly and shifted towards her. "Ever since you came into my life it has been better."

"Awww," Britt cooed. "And you make me better, too."

"And I what you to continue to make my life better." Rich dug into the pocket of his jeans and came out with a ring box from Kay's, and Brittany covered her mouth and gasped, stunned. He cracked open the box, and there sat a diamond-flooded engagement ring. "Brittany, will you make life better for the rest of my days?" he popped the question.

Britt slowly nodded her head. "Yes, Rich! Yes, I will do my all to make your life better than better." Tears of joy sailed down her cheeks as Rich slid the ring on her finger. She then palmed either side of his face and pulled his lips to hers for a deep kiss.

Rich felt that Brittany was right for him so he wanted her in his life for good. He just hoped that he wouldn't lose his life

in the streets and leave her without him. Because Rich understood that Brittany loved him - unlike the streets.

Martell "Troublesome" Bolden

CHAPTER 8

Entering the café, T-Mac surveyed the place for Kat. She had texted him and asked if they could meet up and talk over lunch. And even though he had shit to deal with in the streets, he obliged since he was interested.

Once he noticed Kat, who waved him over to the small table that she occupied, he made his way over to her and took himself a seat. The two admired each other for a moment, their eyes roaming one another before making contact. Just as much as T-Mac thought she was sexy, Kat thought he was fine, and they both knew there was some level of attraction between them.

"Hey, you," Kat greeted him.

"Hey to you, too," T-Mac replied. He leaned forward and rested his folded arms atop the table. "You wanted to talk with me, so what's up?"

"Damn, you get right down to it, huh?"

"Unless you care for foreplay." He smirked.

She blushed and felt herself heat up. "No. I like a nigga who goes right for what he wants."

"Good to know."

"So I want to talk with you about the other day. I didn't expect for you to stand up to Rich for me like that, and I appreciated it," Kat expressed to him.

"That's what standup niggas do. I just thought Rich was bein' a li'l too hard on you, even though you came for Brittany the way you did. Whether you like it or not, he loves her. It's not for you to get in the way of that," T-Mac told her.

"And I'm not trying to get in the way of their love. If Rich wants to be with Brittany, then good for them."

T-Mac detected the attitude in her tone. "You sure that's how you feel? 'Cause it sounds to me like you want Rich for yourself."

"It's not Rich who I want." Kat eyed him through slits. She leaned forward, displaying her bosom in her black fitted Dolce & Gabbana dress, and placed her hand on his. "T-Mac, I just want to be appreciated."

"Look Kat, I'm sure you won't have a problem findin' a nigga to appreciate you. But I'ont think that's me." He withdrew his hand.

"I just want what Shanta had with Don."

"Don was a good nigga for her, unlike that nigga Rob," he said bitterly. "By the way, how is Shan?"

"After all of the trouble in her life with Rob, she's trying to keep it together. Rob really hurt her," she replied.

"Well, Shan won't have to worry about that bitch-ass nigga for long. He's most def' gonna get his for what he did to Don. No cap."

"And I'm sure she will feel better after what Rob put her through."

T-Mac's iPhone chimed and he saw that it was a text from Danger, who was expecting to be scooped up by him. "Gotta go and scoop up Danger. We have some shit to tend to in the streets, so I'ma bounce."

Kat scoffed. She knew Danger liked her, but her feelings wasn't mutual. "Boy, Danger can wait. Before you bounce, why don't you come and appreciate all of this."

"Kat——"

All of a sudden Kat rose to her feet and then strutted her way towards the restroom in her nude Dolce & Gabbana red-bottom heels with T-Mac admiring her round ass in the black body-hugging dress she wore. As she entered the restroom, she looked back over her shoulder at him and used her index finger to seductively coax him to follow her. With no words, T-Mac stood and then followed behind Kat, all the while thinking that Danger would have to wait.

Once he stepped inside the restroom and locked its door, she then threw herself all over him. Kat pushed T-Mac back up against the door and planted kisses on his neck up to his lips while he gripped her round ass in both hands. She reached down, unbuckled his Gucci belt, pulled his hard dick out, then squatted before him and took it into her mouth all the way down to its base while gazing up into his eyes.

He grabbed a fistful of her blonde, long inches of hair as she gave him brain. While fondling T-Mac's balls with her petite hand, Kat worked her mouth on his dick. She sucked its tip as she slid her tongue up and down its shaft. Her full lips and warm tongue felt so fuckin' good to T-Mac as she tasted every inch of him while he fucked her mouth. She sucked and slurped and licked on the dick like a pretty savage. Feeling a nut coming along, T-Mac pulled his dick out of Kat's warm mouth and then jacked its base until he skeeted some sperm in her opened mouth and on her pretty face.

T-Mac pulled Kat up to her feet and then carried her over to the sink, where he sat her atop it. He discovered that she had on no panties as he guided his dick deep inside her wet pussy walls. She spread her legs wide, allowing him to slide every inch of his hardness into her wetness. Her moans of pleasure echoed off the walls of the compact restroom as he bit down on his lower lip while sliding his dick back and forth within in her pussy and she held onto either side of his shoulders. After several thrusts, Kat's pussy became creamy as cum gushed all over T-Mac's stiff dick.

She pushed him back and jumped down to her feet, then turned around and planted her hands on the sink while bent over. He wasted no time pulling up her dress, revealing the huge tattoo of a colorful butterfly on her entire ass, then stuffed his cock inside her slit down to his balls. T-Mac pulled on her hair as he fucked Kat from behind and she arched her back, giving him much more access to dig her out. He liked how she threw it back matching each thrust of his, their flesh made the clapping sound as their skin collided.

T-Mac grunted in pleasure as he felt a nut swell within the tip of dick, and with Kat looking back at it while making fuck-faces, he could no longer resist the inevitable. Pulling his swipe out of her snatch, T-Mac then jacked its base until he squirted semen all over Kat's lower back and her butterfly-tatted ass cheeks. Both appreciated the quick fuck.

"A nigga most def' appreciated all of that." T-Mac smirked as he buckled his Gucci belt.

"I knew you would." Kat smiled as she rearranged her dress.

"Just understand, there's no strings attached."

"Understood. But don't act like you can't talk to a bitch after this, T-Mac." Kat fixed her hair and makeup in the mirror.

"Kat, we ain't gotta talk as long as we know what we both want." T-Mac smacked her on the ass as he made his way out of the restroom, leaving Kat fixing her glamour.

***

Pulling to the curb out front of the trap spot in the hood, T-Mac parked his Porsche truck. He grabbed his iPhone and texted Danger that he was outside, and a moment later, Danger came out carrying a Fendi backpack on his shoulder. After Danger stepped into the passenger seat out of the winter weather, T-Mac pulled off down the street with Lil Baby's "On Me" playing in the background.

"Damn, nigga, fuck took you so long to come scoop me up?" Danger wanted to know.

T-Mac bent the whip at the corner headed northward and said, "Was havin' a talk with Kat."

"And what'd shorty wanna talk with you about?" Danger quirked a brow.

"We didn't do much talkin', feel me?"

"Nigga, stop lyin' on your dick right now!"

"What I gotta lie for? She texted me to meet up with her at a café and when I did, then I ended up givin' her the dick in the restroom. And that bitch can take the dick!" T-Mac told him.

Danger fired up a blunt of za. "I see the bitch ain't text me for no dick," he scoffed and then hit the blunt.

T-Mac glanced over at him and chuckled, "Damn, nigga, sounds to me like you hatin'."

"I'm just sayin' that I been tryna fuck Kat for a while now. And it took you no time to fuck the bitch." Danger had had a thing for Kat for a while and he wanted her, although he understood that if a bitch chooses another nigga, then she wasn't for him. Especially since it was one of his niggas who she chose. He added, "You know it's money over bitches."

"Fa sho'. But enough about that bitch. Is that the work in the backpack?" T-Mac asked as he yielded at a stoplight.

Danger unzipped the backpack and showed him its contents, which was a Draco and two bricks of yae. "We gotta take this work over to Taco Bell and catch a play. And I brought the Drac' along just in case any opp try somethin'," he explained as he pulled the weapon out and sat it on his lap.

"Say no more. With Rich outta town, it's on us to hold shit down," T-Mac expounded.

While Rich was on vacation, T-Mac and Danger were left to hold down the fort. And with all of the beef ongoing, they understood to keep their eyes peeled and their ears to the streets. The two were on their way to catch a play. Afterwards, they would drop by a couple of the trap spots of theirs and collect the profits. Even though they were gettin' to the bag, neither of them would hesitate to bag an opp.

T-Mac pulled the Porsche into the parking lot of Taco Bell and Danger pointed out a parking spot beside the vacant sleek black Mercedes-Benz 650 coup. Before stepping out the whip T-Mac stuffed his Glock .26 with a thirty-shot stick on his waist and Danger replaced the Draco into backpack. As they entered the fast-food joint, T-Mac noticed the buyer seated at a secluded booth, where he was eating a chalupa. T-Mac and Danger made their way over to the booth and slid into the opposite side. While T-Mac did all of the talking, Danger was there for security purposes.

Once the deal was done and the transaction was made, then the buyer exited the restaurant while T-Mac and Danger decided to stay and make an order to go. Afterwards, as they headed towards the Porsche, they were rapping some more about Kat when Danger peeped the familiar Chrysler 300C pull into the restaurant's drive-thru.

"Yo, T-Mac, there's Swindle's whip in the drive-thru," Danger pointed out in a lowered voice. He could make out two silhouettes inside. "Looks like two niggas are inside. I guess it's Swindle and Vito."

T-Mac looked over and saw the Chrysler, then instinctively clutched the butt of his pole. "Since them niggas came for some tacos, I got some shells for they ass."

T-Mac dropped the bag of food on the snow-sheathed ground then pulled his Glock, and Danger pulled the Draco from the backpack that was now filled with cash, then strapped the backpack onto his back. They both gripped their artillery as they began creeping up on the Chrysler from behind. It being afternoon, they had to air out the Chrysler and then flee the scene without any eyewitnesses seeing them. T-Mac and Danger discreetly advanced on the car with their weapons, ready to bust.

Vito, who was in the driver's seat, was placing an order at the loudspeaker when he happened to check the rearview mirror out of habit and peeped T-Mac and Danger creeping up from behind on either side of the Chrysler. And with no hesitation, Vito grabbed up his .9 Taurus, and his shooter in the passenger seat instantly followed suit and gripped his Uzi. Simultaneously, their car doors were pushed opened with Vito hopping out as his shooter followed and both started bustin'.

Blam, blam, blam!

Boc, boc, boc, boc, boc!

Right as Vito and his shooter opened up their heats, T-Mac and Danger ducked out of the way behind an idling SUV, which was also in the drive-thru parallel to the Chrysler, and they opened fire in return. Unfortunately for the driver of the SUV, she was left a casualty of war by rounds that struck her in the chest and neck through the windshield. Taking cover themselves, Vito had hunkered down in front of the Chrysler while his shooter crouched behind its opened passenger door.

T-Mac peeped from behind the SUV and exchanged shots with Vito, bullets narrowly missing both of them. With the Draco in lead, Danger jumped from behind the SUV and let off on Vito's shooter and slugs tore through the door, putting him down. As Danger started to go for Vito the shooter, who was still alive, backed him up while lying on his back shooting at Danger. Then Danger finished the shooter off by filling his chest with slugs.

Vito continued to let off while he attempted to jump back into the Chrysler to make a brazen escape. T-Mac popped Vito twice in the stomach and once in the lower back, which punctured his lung, causing Vito to drop his weapon. Mustering enough strength, Vito stumbled into the Chrysler, then slapped the gear into 'drive' and recklessly skirted off with T-Mac and Danger airing out the car.

The Chrysler only made it a short distance before yielding to a halt in the parking lot. Vito's body lay slumped over once he succumbed to the slugs he'd suffered. This time, Vito wasn't able to escape death.

Immediately, T-Mac and Danger scurried back to the Porsche. As T-Mac fishtailed out of the parking lot, Danger looked around for any signs of Twelve. They had managed to survive the shootout unscathed. Even though they was sure Rich would like to hear that they had hit up Vito, the nigga Swindle was still somewhere hiding out. And T-Mac and Danger knew that Rich wouldn't stop looking for Swindle's ass until he was finally taking a dirt nap.

CHAPTER 9

After pulling into the horseshoe-shaped driveway outside of the mini mansion, which was littered with luxurious vehicles, the Range Rover parked. Rich, along with T-Mac and Danger, had come there to meet with Castle. The meet was to make a re-up. While Rich was out of town on vacay, T-Mac and Danger had made sure all of the work was moved and the money was counted. And soon as Rich returned home, it was back to the money, which came along with problems, although Rich didn't have trouble getting a problem solved with T-Mac and Danger in the equation.

There were three goons posted outside near the front door of the home with artillery on display. After being stripped by Rob and his gang, Castle had beefed up his security because he would never be caught slippin' again. Before stepping out of the Range, Rich placed the .45 holding a thirty-two-shot stick in the pocket of his Monclere jacket, T-Mac strapped his Tec-9 around his neck and concealed it at his side, and Danger stuffed his twin .40s on his waist. It wasn't that they didn't trust Castle; they just trusted that being strapped was best. Rich grabbed up the Fendi backpack filled with the re-up money and stepped out of the whip then T-Mac and Danger followed.

Once Rich, T-Mac, and Danger approached the front door, neither of the armed goons said a word to them nor did they shake the trio down since Castle was expecting them. The goons just led them inside, one in front leading the charge, and two in back trailing the trio.

Upon entering the den, the trio noticed the bullet holes in the walls, which were from the night of Rob's gang pulling the caper. They found Castle sitting perched on a huge desk with Sheik standing right beside him and several more goons present that were also heavily armed. It was as if Castle was the president or some shit; but Rich was there to talk about dead presidents.

"Here's the dope. Show me the money," Castle said, cutting to the chase. He had five individually wrapped bricks sitting out on the desktop.

Rich stepped over to the desk, where he dumped a hundred and twenty-five Gs in stacks of cash atop of it and then replied, "The money is good, but is the dope?"

"Pure cocaine."

"Sounds good." Rich grabbed up each brick and tossed them into the backpack.

Castle looked at the stacks of cash and then to Rich. "You remind me a lot of Don with how you're about your paper."

"What can I say? Bro taught me the game."

"And the game cold, but it's fair. Even still, sometimes it's necessary to get even."

"Soon as I find Rob, then I'll get even once his body drops."

"I know where to find his ass. And once he shows his face, then he'll be dead," Castle assured.

"How'd you find his ass?" Rich wanted to know.

"A bitch will always be a nigga's downfall if he's not careful." He knew that all too well after Parker had led Rob to him. "Rob's layin' low at a bitch name Trina crib out in the Meadows. But li'l do he know, I got shooters lurkin' outside of her crib."

"Well, if you don't body his ass, then I surely will. The shit he did to my bro can't go unanswered."

"Look, I know you would rather be the one to body Rob for what he did to Don. But that nigga took my fuckin' money and almost took my damn life, so I want his ass just as bad. Just look at it like this: whichever one of us gets him first, let's keep in mind it's for both of us. Feel me?" Castle expounded.

"Yeah, I feel you. So I'll be sure to bust two in his top—one for me and one for you," Rich swore.

"Two in the top will dead him fa sho'." Castle grabbed another brick, then handed it over to Rich and told him, "This one's on the strength of Don. Just make sure you stay ahead of the game."

Rich put the extra brick inside the backpack with the others. "Only way to stay ahead of the game is to run it."

Subsequent to leaving Castle's place, the trio were in traffic on the way to their hood. Rich took up the backseat with the backpack beside him while T-Mac rode shotgun and Danger pushed the Range over the snow-sheathed street. They all had their eyes peeled for cops and robbers on their tail. Young Dolph's tune "Coordinate" played in the background.

During the ride, Rich held thoughts about Castle mentioning having found where Rob was hiding out at. Rich couldn't help but think about killing Rob himself to avenge his brother, although he didn't want to let his thirst for vengeance get in the way of gettin' to the bag. But he wanted to put Rob in the dirt, even if it was the last thing he did. Rich hit the blunt of cookie weed and mused, *On bro's grave, Rob's ass is good as dead.*

"Yo Rich, you gonna pass the blunt or what?" Danger said, snapping Rich out of his thoughts.

"Yeah. My bad," Rich responded and then went to pass him the blunt which T-Mac intercepted.

"You worried about the wrong shit right now, Danger," T-Mac told him. He puffed the blunt and eyed Rich through the rearview mirror. "Rich, what's on your mind?"

Rich leaned forward in his seat. "Murder's on my mind. I wanna drop Rob's bitch ass before Castle get the chance to."

"What does it matter who offs the nigga as long as he's dead?" Danger commented as he yielded the Range to a halt at a stoplight on Humboldt & Burleigh Street.

T-Mac cut his eyes at him and said, "Danger, it matters 'cause it's personal. I get that Rob took shit from Castle, but that nigga took Don from us."

"And there's no doubt I'm willin' to slide on Rob outta love for Don. Either way, I just wanna see his ass dead is all," Danger expressed.

"Indeed." T-Mac puffed the blunt once more then passed it to Danger. "'Cause you definitely didn't have a problem slidin' on Vito."

"Been wantin' to slide on Vito any-fuckin'-way." Danger inhaled the weed smoke, then exhaled a thick cloud.

Rich leaned back in his seat and said, "Good thing Vito's dead, but I'd rather it be Swindle." He had been informed of them killing Vito, but it was Swindle who he wanted dead more. "But don't trip. We gon' slide on Rob and Swindle. And I want both of 'em to die hard. 'Til we get the chance to slide on them niggas, we'll flip these bricks and chase a check."

As bad as Rich wanted to slide on Rob and Swindle, he knew there was still money to be made. He knew that T-Mac and Danger were down for whatever, but Rich needed them both to assist him with running the game. Because together, they were a force to be reckoned with.

***

"Shan, what's taking you so damn long? Is everything okay in there, bitch?" Kat called out to Shanta, who had been locked in the bathroom for a moment.

The girls were at Shanta's place. It was early in the morning and Kat was there as moral support. Shan needed her friend in that moment. It would have been nice if Parker could be there also, she felt. She was both scared and anxious while awaiting to learn whether or not she was with child after having morning sickness for a week. Shanta didn't know what she would do if so.

"It's been ten minutes already. Are you preg—" Kat's words were cut once Shan pulled open the bathroom door and she could see on Shan's face that something was a matter. "You okay?"

Shanta held up the pregnancy test and stammered, "I'm... I'm pregnant."

"Girl, I don't know if I should be happy or sad for you right now." Kat ushered Shan over to the couch in the front room, where they took a seat.

"What am I going to do? Can't believe that I'm pregnant by Rob, when he's the one who killed Don," Shan sobbed as tears streamed down her cheeks. Never could she have imagined being in such a bizarre position. In between losing her unborn child by Don to the hands of Rob whose unborn child she was now carrying, Shan felt like she was trapped in a bad dream.

Kat stood and said, "What you need right about now is a drink." She headed to retrieve a bottle of wine from the adjacent kitchen.

"Kat, I'm sitting here pregnant. I shouldn't be drinking, no matter how bad I do need it," Shan protested.

"Then how about I have a drink for the both us, because girl, I need it just as much." Kat returned sipping from the bottle and took her seat beside Shanta. "So, what're going to do?"

"I-I don't know. On the one hand I don't feel it'll be right for me to keep the baby just because it's Rob's. On the other hand, I don't feel it'll be right to get rid of the baby just because it's not Don's," she expounded.

Kat gingerly rubbed her friend's arm in comfort. "Shanta, whatever you choose to do then as your bestie, I will support you all the way. All I'm going to tell you is just please don't make a choice that you'll regret for the rest of your life solely based upon your feelings towards either Rob or Don. Girl, make a choice that you feel is best for you in life," she expressed sincerely.

"Thanks Kat. I appreciate your support. It would be nice if Parker was here with us so she could give me her advice as well."

"She is here with us in spirit. And knowing Parker, sis would want you to choose what's best for you."

"Sounds about right," Shan concurred. "I still can't believe she got with the wrong man in Castle. Why do us women pick the wrong men most times?"

"Good question. That's why I don't pick niggas who I don't see myself with," Kat replied.

Shanta shifted in her seat towards Kat and eyed her through slits. "And what about T-Mac? He's a good dude and all, but do you see yourself with him?"

Kat turned the bottle up to her lips. "Damn. Now you all up in my business and shit. Knew I shouldn't have told your ass about me and T-Mac. Look, it was just one date we spent together so I can't say whether I see myself with him long-term. But a bitch wouldn't mind going back for seconds."

"Girl, you know he's Don's and Rich's favorite cousin. And Angie treats him like a son. Also he's practically family to me just as much you are. So I don't want either of you to wound up hurt. I'm not saying don't see T-Mac anymore. I'm just saying make sure you and he have an understanding."

"I hear you, Shan. And I will be careful with T-Mac. He's a sweet dude and I like that about him. But enough about my relationship goals," Kat said. She changed the subject. "Back to you and the pregnancy. You definitely need to choose what you're going to do about the baby before it's too late. So think on that."

Shanta sat back in her seat with her hands over her still flat belly and, in a lowered voice, she replied, "This isn't about Rob or Don. It's about me."

Shanta's feelings for both men was strong in different ways. But of course, after learning that Rob had a part in killing Don, Shanta felt indifferent towards Rob. But how could she punish an innocent unborn child due to it being Rob's? Then again, how could she even consider having the child since it wasn't Don's? She had a dilemma – one that she would have to think about long and hard.

***

While snuggled up in bed, Rich and Brittany were watching reruns of *Martin*. It was only afternoon and they were smoking on a blunt of exotic weed and laughing their asses off at the comical TV show. Ever since being back from their vacay, Rich wanted to find more time to chill with Britt whenever he could. He realized that she was all he needed. Thus far, no one else was aware of their engagement, although he looked forward to marrying her.

Rich's iPhone began to vibrate on the nightstand. He reached over and grabbed up the phone then noticed it was a FaceTime call from his mom, Angie. Swiping the phone's touchscreen display with a finger allowed Rich to answer the call. "'Sup, Ma?"

"Hey, son. And Brittany," Angie replied, seeing Brittany right beside him. He could tell she was home by her background.

"Hi, Angie!" Brittany responded and waved at her. "Look, I'll leave you two be." She pecked Rich's lips then slid out of bed and headed for the adjacent bathroom.

"How're things with you and Brittany?"

"Better than ever so far. She makes me happy."

"That's good! Any babies in the near future?" Angie pressed.

"Not right now, Ma," Rich chuckled. "But I do got somethin' to share with you."

"Since it's been a while, how about you just come by for Sunday dinner? Then we'll be able to spend some time together while we talk," she suggested.

"My bad, Ma. Shoulda made a stop by your place once I got back from out of town. I'll be sure to drop by with Britt on Sunday."

"Sounds good. And I'll also invite Shanta since it's been a while that she was last with us. Been since Don passed. I haven't seen her lately, but the last time I did I could tell that she was still grieving. I wonder how she's holding up now."

Rich sat up in bed. "Ma, there's somethin' you should know about Shan," he said in a lowered voice.

"What is it, Rich?" Angie could read on his face that something was a matter. "Is Shanta alright?"

"Well, yeah, she's alright. But..." Rich thought twice about telling his mom that Shanta had been with Don's killer. He just didn't want Angie to have something more to stress over. Besides, from his understanding, Shan wasn't aware of who Rob was whenever she first met him, so it wasn't like she was with him on purpose. If only Rich knew that Shanta was pregnant by Rob.

Angie spoke up. "Richard, you can tell me whatever it is."

"It's just Shanta is still takin' the loss of Don hard," he said instead.

"I think we all are. So, it'll be good for Shan to be with us come Sunday so she can feel our love and support. It's what Don would want of us," she responded. "Rich, you know Don was always proud to have you as his brother."

"Yeah, I know. That's why I just can't let anyone involved in what happened to him live. Especially Swindle."

"Whatever you do, just be careful. I don't want to lose you too, Rich."

"Ma, you won't lose me," Rich assured.

Brittany returned to the bedroom. She slid into bed beside Rich as he and Angie ended the call with plans to see each other during Sunday's dinner. It was obvious to Britt how close he and Angie had grown ever since Don's death. Brittany just cared to be embraced by their family with open arms. She wondered how Angie would react once learning of hers and Rich's engagement.

"Is everything okay with your mom?" Britt wanted to know.

Rich set his phone back on the nightstand. "Yeah. She just wanted to check in on me. Said she wants us to come over for dinner on Sunday."

"That sounds like a plan. Did you happen to tell her about our engagement?"

"No, I figured it'll be better to announce it durin' the dinner."

"Well, I just hope she will be happy for us."

"Don't worry, baby. She will be," Rich told her. "Now, lay back in my arms."

As they lay in bed, Rich thought about his mom's concerns about losing him too. He knew he needed to be there for her. And peering down at Brittany, Rich also wanted to be there for her. He understood that he had to ride on his enemies. His enemies were the difference between life and death.

CHAPTER 10

"Where do you think you're going?" Trina asked once Rob stepped into the front room, where she was seated on the couch.

"I need to go to the graveyard," Rob told her as he stuffed his FN in the waistline of his RockStar jeans. After being holed up in her apartment for the past few weeks while he healed, Rob was ready to go and collect his buried away money.

Trina used the remote to turn off the TV. "Why the graveyard, Rob?" she asked, curious.

"Trina, don't ask questions. Just do as I say and take me to where I need to go."

"Are you sure that you want to chance going out with Castle looking for you?"

"I ain't duckin' Castle or no nigga. Besides, I can't stay in the crib forever. Sooner or later they may learn I'm here, so it's best that I just give 'em what they're lookin' for."

"But Rob—"

"No buts, Trina. Now either you can go out with me, or I'll go out by myself," he demanded.

"Don't say I didn't warn you," she huffed as she headed to dress herself in something comfortable.

It was later in the evening and being the wintertime, the weather was frosty and the sky was darkened. Rob remained standing in front of the complex while surveilling the block as Trina made her way to her whip that was parked across the street. Once Trina was inside the Jaguar, she turned over the engine, then pulled into the middle of the street. Seeing nothing out of the ordinary, Rob made his way towards the whip, then suddenly a parked car's blinding headlights flicked on, and three gunmen jumped out.

"Just give up Castle's money and maybe I'll let you live," Sheik forewarned with two shooters flanking him.

"Then good thing I got this FN 'cause I'ont have Castle's money," Rob retorted as he went for his weapon.

Rrraaa, rrraaa, rrraaa!

As automatic gunfire erupted from Sheik's MK-18, Rob had ducked beside the whip and pulled his own gun. He had just barely evaded being struck down by slugs. His heart raced as bullets continued to be fired at him, some peppering the vehicle. It was no surprise to him that the shooters belonged to none other than Castle.

Rob sprayed his FN over the hood of the whip and dropped one of the three gunmen. He noticed Trina was slumped to the side dead in the driver's seat from catching slugs from the shooters in her forehead and chest through the front windshield.

While Sheik and the other shooter sent shots at him, Rob hurriedly made his way to the driver's side of the idling car. He then snatched open the door and pulled Trina's dead body up out of it, using her frame as a shield while he shot back at the shooters.

Trina's corpse was riddled with bullets, protecting Rob from being shot. As the two shooters advanced on him, Rob popped at Sheik, causing him to dive onto the snow covered pavement.

Rob then tossed Trina's dead body aside before jumping in the whip and skirting off down the street. Keeping his head low, he avoided being hit up as the standing shooter fired shots into the front windshield. Going full speed, Rob crashed into the gunman, who flew onto the hood of the car and forcefully slammed against the windshield, smashing it. The gunman was left in critical condition once he hit the pavement while Rob continued speeding away.

Though Rob had managed to escape the shooters with his life, he knew that he would have to either kill Castle or get out of town, because the shooters wouldn't stop gunning after him if not. But at the moment, he needed to find somewhere that he wouldn't be found, and he knew just the place.

***

Kayla sat on the couch in the front room of her place drinking a glass of wine while watching *Real Housewives of Atlanta*. Tonight, she just wanted to chillax. It didn't feel the same her being home alone without TJ there, but she just had to get used to it now that he was dead and gone. Although she had to admit that she felt so alone - so much so that she even thought about calling over Bone to keep her company.

Grabbing up her iPhone from the end table, Kayla scrolled its number log until coming across Bone's number. *Here goes nothing,* she mused as she started to press "call". But Kayla was stopped when there came a knock at her front door. She wasn't expecting any company so she didn't know who it could be. Part of her hoped it was none other than Bone.

Rising to her feet, Kayla made her way over to the door. "Who is it?"

"Kayla, it's me. Rob."

"Rob?" Kayla pulled open the door and couldn't believe that Rob was standing there. She immediately noticed the scar left on his face.

"Mind if I come in?" Rob said urgently.

"Come on in." She stepped aside and allowed him inside of the loft, then locked the door behind him. "I... I thought you was dead."

"No. Niggas just wish I was dead," Rob replied. "I just been layin' low ever since shit went wrong on that lick. And

I'm sorry about TJ. I know losin' him is hard on you as much as it is on me."

Kayla sat on the couch. "Yeah. I'm still trying to cope with the loss of TJ. He was my everything," she said, growing choked up.

"I know. For whatever it's worth, you still have me."

"That means a lot to me, Rob. But what I don't understand is how are you still living when Bone told me that he was the only one who made it out alive?"

Rob removed the FN from his waist and set it atop the end table before he took a seat on the arm of the couch. "Bone told you that, huh? Well, that's what he thinks, 'cause he betrayed us. Bone let TJ get killed on that lick. He was the one who finished off Max, and he shot me in the fuckin' face in an attempt to leave me for dead, all so he could take the money for himself. Bone ain't to be trusted," he expounded in rage.

"Oh my God!" Kayla gasped because she never thought that Bone was capable of such treachery. "Bone came here and gave me some money that he claimed was on the strength of TJ. Now I realize that he was just trying to get to me while I was vulnerable. And I can't believe it almost worked. If anyone should be dead, it's Bone."

"Then we'll make sure he's a dead man," Rob declared. "But for now, I'll need a place to lay low. I can't go back to where I was 'cause it's no longer safe for me there with the nigga that we robbed havin' shooters after me."

"Of course! You can stay here for as long as you need to, Rob."

"Don't worry, I won't stay for long."

"Then where are you going to go with no money?"

"Money ain't an issue. Once I catch Bone slippin', then I'll make his ass give up the money he took. Afterwards, I'll get outta town," Rob explained. He was sure that Bone still had most of the money from the lick on Castle, and he planned to have Bone take him to it and then leave him dead. Not to mention Rob still had the buried away money in the grave.

Kayla looked to him with inquiring eyes. "Do you really think you'll be able to kill Bone?"

Rob nodded his assurance. "I'll kill Bone when he least expects it."

"And I want nothing more than to see Bone killed." She polished off the remains of her glass of wine then stood. "Look, I'm going to get ready for bed. Make yourself at home and if you need anything, just let me know." She made her way into the bedroom.

Peering down at the FN, Rob couldn't help but think about it sparing his life earlier tonight. He regretted that he wasn't able to spare Trina. And killing Castle would be vindication. But first, Rob had to put a bullet in Bone.

Martell "Troublesome" Bolden

CHAPTER 11

Parking at the curb before Angie's place, Shanta along with Kat sat in her Nissan Altima. She let out a sigh then said, "I don't know if I'm ready to see Don's family."

"Girl, I'm here with you as support. But if you don't want to go inside, then we can just leave," Kat responded.

"No, I think it's best that I go in. Besides, I don't care to be rude by not showing up after I promised Angie that I would. It's just..."

"Just what, Shan?"

"Nothing." Shanta didn't want to bring up her pregnancy in that moment.

Kat shifted towards her. "Listen." She put a hand on Shan's arm in comfort. "Let's just go in and enjoy ourselves."

"Thanks for being here with me, girl. Here goes nothing."

Shanta and Kat aborted the car then made their way to the house through the snowfall. After ringing the doorbell, a moment later Angie answered the door and greeted them before allowing them inside.

"Nice to see you. Glad you could come," Angie addressed Shan and offered her a hug.

"I had to come see you. And I hope you don't mind me bringing my girl, Kat, along," Shanta replied.

"No, I don't mind at all. The more the merrier. Nice to meet you, Kat."

"Likewise," Kat replied.

"I made more than enough food for everyone. How about we go in the dining room with the others?" Angie led the way to the dining room with the girls in tow.

Upon entering the dining room, they came upon Rich, Brittany, and T-Mac, who were all seated around the beautifully-set dining room table that was dressed with food. Angie out did herself on this dinner.

Rich stood and offered Shanta a hug and disregarded Kat. "What's up, sis? Good to see you."

"You too, bro." Shanta took the seat that he pulled out for her. "Hey, Brittany."

"Hey to you too, Shanta." Brittany cut her eyes to Kat, whom she didn't like much. "Kat."

Kat just offered a half-wave as she sat beside Shan. She looked over at T-Mac and a smile appeared on her full lips, and he couldn't help but smirk. It was apparent that they liked each other more than they led on.

"It's nice to have all of you here. I know we haven't had Sunday dinner since Don has been gone, and we all been going through our own trials. But it's best that we come together on the strength of Don and show each other love," Angie said.

"It's what Don would want," Rich added. "And since we're all here, I have a big announcement to make. Me and Britt are now engaged to be married." He held up Brittany's hand to proudly show off the rock on her ring finger. "And I wish Don could be here to celebrate our love, but I know he would be happy for us."

"Of course, Don would be happy for you, Rich. I'm sure we all are," Shan input. She discretely nudged Kat with an elbow when she scoffed.

Angie reached over and cupped her son's cheek. "I couldn't be any happier because Brittany is perfect for you. And now maybe you two will give me some grandbabies!"

"Ma, let us have our weddin' before we think about havin' some babies," Rich replied.

"I think we'll make some cute babies together," Britt chimed in.

All of the talk about babies made Shanta uncomfortable. She didn't know if she should mention to them that she was pregnant, especially after losing Don's unborn child. *How can I explain to them that I'm pregnant by the man who killed Don?* she contemplated. Then she decided it was in her best interest to keep it to herself for now.

"How about we go ahead and enjoy this good food?" Rich encouraged.

After Angie said grace, everyone dug into the home-cooked meal. There was mac & cheese, fried chicken, mashed potatoes, coleslaw, pinto beans, buttermilk biscuits, and different desserts. The aroma filled the room and the food was delicious, not to mention they all had glasses of wine, with the exception of Shanta. They held trivial conversation over their meals.

"Shan, I noticed you haven't touched your drink," Angie pointed out.

Shanta seemed a bit blindsided. "Yeah, um, I'm just trying to cut back on drinking. A girl gotta know her limits," she replied, hoping Angie would buy it, because she wasn't quite ready to reveal her pregnancy.

"Whatever's best for you." Angie didn't think twice about it.

"Well, good for you, but more for me," Kat chimed in and grabbed Shanta's glass of wine for herself.

Following dinner, Angie and the girls were in the kitchen cleaning. Rich and T-Mac were standing outside in the cold weather on the front porch sharing a blunt of cookie weed.

"Congrats on your engagement, cuz," T-Mac said.

"'Preciate it. I just wish Don was here to be part of the ceremony," Rich uttered.

T-Mac looked to him. "Listen, Don's watchin' over you. So trust me, he'll be part of it in spirit."

"I guess you're right." Rich puffed the blunt then said, "Cuz, I want you to be my best man. You always had my back and I trust you with my life. So I think it's best to have you by my side on one of the biggest days of my life."

"I'd be honored to be your best man. But you know Danger is gonna be jealous. How 'bout you make him the ring bearer," T-Mac cracked and they shared a laugh.

"Don't worry. I'll make sure Danger is a groomsman."

"I'm sure Danger will be honored. Maybe we shoulda made him come here with us tonight."

"I invited him to come. But it was Danger's choice to tend to shit in the streets instead. I think bein' here woulda reminded him too much of Don and C-note, since they used to all come here every Sunday."

"Rich, we gotta do everything we can to get revenge for what happened to Don and C-note. Even if it kills us."

Rich hit the weed then exhaled a thick cloud of smoke. "And we will. First we gotta find Swindle and Rob. Whenever we do, then they're good as dead," he assured. He passed the blunt back to T-Mac.

Shanta and Kat emerged from the house with plates of food covered in saran wrap that Angie insisted they take home. When Rich asked to speak with Shan alone, T-Mac decided to walk Kat to the car parked near the curb.

"How you holdin' up? You seemed a lil distracted durin' dinner," Rich had noticed.

Shanta let out a sigh. "It was just all the talk about marriage and babies started to get to me. You know, it reminded me of everything I lost with Don."

"I understand. It must be very hard on you. Especially when you can't get any of it back."

"I almost started not to show up tonight. I just didn't want to see you and your mom and feel guilty about being with Rob."

"Look, of course I hate the thought of you gettin' with Rob. But it's not like you got with the nigga knowin' who he was in the first place. So you ain't guilty of shit. Besides, I'ma kill that nigga, Rob, for takin' away Don and your unborn child," he vowed.

In that moment Shanta didn't know how to tell Rich about her pregnancy. But she felt the need to. "Rich, I..." She couldn't seem to get the words out.

"What's good, sis?" he urged.

"I'm happy for you and Brittany," she said instead. "Just treat her right."

"Thanks. I will." Rich watched as Shanta waltzed to her car. He felt there was something going on with her but he had no idea as to what. "Don't think I didn't notice how you and Kat were all over each other," he pointed out as T-Mac stepped up on the porch.

"Kat and I are just cool," T-Mac replied.

"What's that all about?"

"She and I been smashin'. Started while you were outta town on vacay. And shorty got some good pussy!" T-Mac exclaimed.

"Good thing she's on your dick now instead of mine. Keep it up and you'll be the one engaged next."

"Nigga, please. I'ma be a playa for life." He puffed the blunt and then passed it to Rich. "Look, I'ma head to the crib. Let Aunt Angie know that I enjoyed the dinner. And I'll be sure to show up next Sunday."

"Have a safe ride to the crib."

T-Mac patted the Glock on his waist. "Safety first."

The two dapped before T-Mac turned for his Porsche truck parked in the driveway. As T-Mac pulled away, Rich puffed the blunt once more, then flicked it away before heading back inside the home to spend time with his mother and fiancée.

***

T-Mac zipped the Porsche truck through the night traffic while bangin' Rod Wave's tune "Rags2Riches". He braked at the stoplight on 35th and Hampton Street. For safety measures, he gripped the pole in his lap and surveilled his surroundings for signs of anything amiss.

With all the beef in the streets, T-Mac didn't plan to be caught slippin'. He understood they needed to find Swindle and Rob and then off them both so they wouldn't have to look over their shoulders as much. After smokin' Vito, T-Mac knew that was one less opp they had to watch their backs for. However, T-Mac realized there were many niggas looking to stab them in their backs if given the chance.

Once the light turned green, T-Mac zipped off, going eastbound on Hampton Street. He checked the rearview mirror out of habit and peeped an unmarked police car coming up the rear. The unmarked car's lights flickered looking for the Porsche to pull over.

"Shit," T-Mac cursed in frustration. He was ridin' dirty with the pole on him, and he didn't want to be caught with it. So instead of pulling over, T-Mac sped off, taking Twelve on a high-speed chase.

Running through a red light, T-Mac nearly caused a collision with crossing traffic. He wove the Porsche through vehicles as he tried shaking the unmarked car that was closely on his tail. Next thing he knew, there was a backup unit joining the chase. T-Mac figured Twelve had to be after him for a reason since they seemed eager to stop him. However, he refused to be stopped by the law, knowing how most cops have no regards for Black lives as if they don't matter.

The cruiser collided into the side of the Porsche in attempt to put a stop to the chase. Up ahead there were stop sticks laid out in the street, and as T-Mac rolled over the spikes, the tires of the Porsche were shredded, causing the SUV to spin out of control and then crash into a light pole.

The airbags had deployed, but that wasn't enough to prevent T-Mac from slamming his head against the steering wheel, which caused a laceration across the forehead. He was a bit disoriented, and his head was spinning. Once regaining his composure, T-Mac realized there were cops surrounding the Porsche with their service weapons drawn. The cops moved in on him with their guns leveled and one of them pulled T-Mac out of the Porsche onto the snow-sheathed pavement and then cuffed him behind the back.

"You're under arrest for first degree intentional murder," the US Marshal announced before reading T-Mac his Miranda rights.

Unbeknownst to T-Mac, he was wanted by the authorities for the murder of Vito.

CHAPTER 12

Kayla pulled open the front door wearing a red silk negligée and nothing beneath it with a pair of red patent leather Christian Dior stilettos, and Bone liked what he saw. She grabbed him by his Balenciaga polo shirt and pulled him inside of the loft. He noticed the lights were down low, making for a romantic setting.

Unexpectedly, Bone had received a text earlier from Kayla for him to come see her. He'd never really gotten over her even after she decided to get with TJ. Part of him always believed that he could have Kayla back, even if that meant TJ had to meet his demise. Anyway, Bone always felt that Kayla should have been his. And now that he had the opportunity to get with her, there was nothing that could stop him. The whole drive to Kayla's place Bone couldn't help but think about how he would fuck her, and tonight he had it in mind to fuck her better than TJ ever did.

"I knew you'd eventually hit me up," Bone said. "Been waitin' on you."

"And I'm worth the wait," Kayla replied seductively.

Bone pulled her close to him at the waist. "For all those years I was on lockdown, I thought about fuckin' you again. To keep shit real, I know I acted as if it didn't, but you gettin' with TJ bothered me."

"Bone, I never stopped wanting you. What I had with TJ was nothing like what I had with you. I just didn't know how to tell him my true feelings."

"But now he's out of the picture, so me and you can get back together."

"I'd like that. Now take me to the room and fuck me," Kayla demanded.

Bone picked Kayla up by her ass and hauled her into the bedroom, where the lights were completely off. He laid her back on the bed and she grabbed the pistol from his waist and set it atop the nightstand. Bone pushed Kayla back in bed and spread her legs, revealing her bare pussy. He then knelt between her agape legs and began licking Kayla's clitoris. She palmed his head and encouraged him to eat her.

While Bone was preoccupied eating Kayla's pussy, Rob crept out of the closet where he had been in wait, hiding with his Glock.

Unbeknownst to Bone, Kayla had called him over to set his ass up for Rob. She was disgusted by Bone and didn't want him near her at all. And to hear him say the shit he had said about TJ made her hate Bone more than she thought she could. All she wanted was for Bone to be killed on the strength of TJ.

Rob cocked back the slide of the Glock, which instantly had gotten Bone's attention, who looked up at Rob wide-eyed. Right then Bone realized that Kayla had set him up for Rob to kill.

What the hell? Bone contemplated, trying to register seeing Rob alive.

"What's the matter, Bone? Look like you seen a ghost," he smirked while targeting Bone's top.

"Not a ghost; just a dead man walkin'," Bone retorted.

Rob chuckled. "I ain't the one with the gun aimed in my face this time around, if you haven't noticed."

"But I did notice the scar that the slug left in your face there." Bone peeped that the bullet wound in Rob's jaw had healed in a disfiguring way.

"I can live with a scar. But you'll be dead." Rob understood that a dead man can't pay so he needed to get the money first. "Where's the fuckin' money, Bone?"

Bone scoffed. "Rob, I'll take that to the grave. Matter fact, how about I also just take all of the money in the grave you have buried away after I kill you?"

"Not unless I kill your ass first."

"Nigga—" He started to stand from in between Kayla's legs until Rob halted him.

"Stay on your fuckin' knees. That way you can pray to the man above and beg Him for mercy."

"Rob, one thing for sure, I ain't beggin' no one for mercy."

Rob shook his damn head. "And after how you betrayed me, TJ, and Max, I'ont plan to show you any mercy. The difference between me and you is I'ma make sure you're dead."

Suddenly, Bone made a swift maneuver and grabbed his own Glock from the nightstand as he ducked beside the bed. Then he and Rob matched guns.

Blocka, blocka, blocka, blocka!

Boom, boom, boom!

Bullets whizzed by Rob and Bone only inches away as they busted at each other. Rob fell backwards into the closet during his attempt to dodge being popped while still bustin' at Bone. Bone seized the opportunity to flee as he busted back at Rob over his shoulder on his way hurrying out the room. They both managed to avoid being shot. However, Kayla had been caught in the crossfire and was riddled with several bullets that left her clinging on to dear life.

Rob hurried to his feet with his gun in hand. He checked on Kayla's wellness. She was sprawled on the bed bleeding to death and gasping for air, and seeing the quarter-sized bullet holes in her chest, Rob knew she was a goner. Now Bone was responsible for Kayla and TJ losing their lives. How the fuck did he let Bone slip away? Rob knew he had to catch Bone before it was too late and kill his ass. He rushed out of the loft after Bone.

Bone hurried out of the complex, headed for his whip with his gun in hand. He couldn't believe that Kayla had tried setting him up, so he didn't feel bad about filling her with bullets on his way out. *Now she can be with TJ*, he thought menacingly. Then there was Rob. Bone was lucky to have evaded being killed by him. He regretted not making sure Rob's ass was dead the night he had shot him back at the Diamond Inn. Now he knew it was either him or Rob.

As Rob came rushing out of the complex, he caught Bone as he was just about jump into his Yukon. With no hesitation Rob fired at him then Bone turned firing back. Flames spit from both of their gun's muzzles while they ducked out of the way of the deadly fire. Bone jumped in the whip and then sped off down the street with Rob decorating the vehicle with bullet holes until it wildly turned out of sight.

***

"Damn it," Bone cursed in frustration and slammed his fist down against the steering wheel as he sped away. He was very aware that since Rob was somehow still alive, then Rob would gun after him relentlessly. Therefore, it was in his best interest to go at Rob with guns blazing. And Bone knew just who could assist his motive.

Bone sped the entire way to see Swindle all while perpetually checking his rearview mirror. He figured that Swindle would be willing to assist him in getting rid of Rob for the good of them both.

After parking the Yukon, Bone stepped out and couldn't help but notice the numerous bullet holes in the vehicle, and he knew that he was lucky to be alive. He just hated that Rob was still alive also. Bone approached the front door and knocked. His head was on the swivel for anything amiss as he awaited an answer.

"Hell are you doin' here?" Swindle asked once he opened the door and found Bone. He gripped his gun.

"I'm here 'cause I need your assistance," Bone told him.

Stepping aside, Swindle allowed Bone inside. The two made their way into the front room. Bone saw there was lots of cash spread out on the coffee table. Swindle had been interrupted while counting up some profits. They took a seat on the couch.

"What is it you need my assistance with?" Swindle wanted to know as he went back to adding up his funds.

"More like who. It's Rob," Bone informed.

Swindle shot him a look. "Rob? Thought that nigga was dead."

"And I thought the same. But after I left the nigga for dead, somehow he managed to live."

"And how do you know that he's still alive?"

Bone scoffed. "'Cause he just tried to dead me when I least expected it. I was lucky to make it out alive my-damn-self. Can't believe I just seen Rob still breathin'."

"Seein' is believin'," Swindle told him.

"Then I wanna see Rob dead with my own two eyes," Bone replied menacingly. "And I'm sure you need to see the same. 'Cause we both know if Rob finds out that you put me up to betrayin' him, then he'll have it out for you too."

"Instead of implyin' what I think you're implyin', if you need me to assist you in seein' to it that Rob's dead for sure, then that's all you have to say. Don't trip; I got your back." He really only gave a fuck about watching his own back.

"Good to know." Bone stood to his feet. "If you're lookin' for me, then I'll be layin' low at the Diamond Inn until I find a way to kill Rob. I'm sure it's the last place he'll look to find me. I'll be in touch."

Swindle locked the door behind Bone after his departure. He returned to his seat on the couch with thoughts of his talk with Bone on his mind. And he couldn't help but think about Rob still being alive after Bone was supposed to have killed him. He had to admit that Bone was right. If Rob found out that he had a part in Bone's betrayal, then Swindle would certainly become a bigger target for Rob. So Swindle understood he had to assist Bone in getting rid of Rob if he wanted to live without having to watch his back, because he rather watch his money pile up. Matter fact, he put his mind on the money and went back to calculating his profits.

***

Rob needed to get off the streets following the shootout with Bone. He made his way to his place, where he would duck off and plan his next move. Now that Bone was aware he was still alive, he knew that Bone would eventually come gunning for him along with the rest. So it was best that he find Bone first in order to kill him. And Rob knew just how to go about it.

Entering his place, Rob locked the door behind himself. He hadn't been there in weeks and needed to grab a few things. But he realized that he couldn't stay there for too long because Bone was sure to come there gunning for him. His plan was to ultimately collect the money in the grave which he had buried away and then skip town. But before following through with his plan, Rob wanted to see to it that Bone was dead.

Rob stepped into his bedroom. He made his way over to the nightstand and pulled open the top drawer. Inside there was a bulk of jewelry that he had stripped niggas for during previous licks. He grabbed up Swindle's chain. Since he planned to go and see Swindle, the chain is what he would use as an incentive to possibly get Swindle to talk. Rob figured if anyone knew where to find Bone, then it would be Swindle, because he was sure that Bone had gone to Swindle to sell him the keys from the lick on Castle. And part of Rob's plan was to make sure Castle got what he had coming. Rob understood that he had a lot working in his favor to be the last nigga standing.

Seeing Don's Rolex timepiece inside of the drawer caused Rob to think about Shanta. He had to admit that he still held feelings for her. But he was sure that she didn't want a thing to do with him after she had learned that he had a part in Don being murked. Rob never meant to hurt Shan, and he wanted to make amends with her. But how? Maybe it was best that he forget all about her and just leave town with his money.

Rob grabbed a Chanel backpack from the closet, then placed the chain along with a few other essential items inside. He packed light so it wouldn't be a problem for him getting out of town after getting rid of Bone. But for the next few days, Rob would lay low at his place until he was ready to make his next move.

Martell "Troublesome" Bolden

CHAPTER 13

While sitting in the waiting area of the clinic, Shanta's stomach was in a knots. She was nervous about getting an abortion. Part of her didn't know if she wanted to keep the baby or get rid of it. How could she birth Rob's child, knowing that he was the reason as to why she had lost her and Don's unborn child? Although she wasn't quite ready to lose another child for any reason. So at this point, Shanta wasn't sure if it was best for her to go through with the procedure or not. Whichever, she didn't want to regret her choice for the rest of her life.

"Girl, are you okay?" Kat asked, noticing that her girl was a nervous wreck. She was there with Shan as moral support.

"No, I'm not okay. I don't know if I should go through with the abortion," Shan answered, her voice low.

"Well, I won't encourage you nor discourage you to do anything. All I'll say is you need to make the best choice for you."

"That's the thing. I don't want to regret whichever choice I make."

Kat shifted towards Shan in her seat. "Honestly, either way, I believe you will regret making a choice. I know it's not easy for you to have Rob's baby after losing Don's the unfortunate way you did. Although I also know it's not easy for you to choose to lose another baby. Shan, whichever choice you make today, just be ready to live with it," she expounded.

"How can I live with having the man's child who took away Don's child? Then again, how can I live with knowing I chose to abort an innocent child? Then there's Rich and his mom. I don't want them to resent me if I choose to keep Rob's baby," Shan expressed.

"Have you made your mind up on whether or not you're going to tell Rich?"

"First and foremost, I need to make mind up on whether or not I will go through with this procedure. Afterwards, I'll think about telling Rich about the pregnancy."

"Girl, you know I will support whichever choice you make. And you shouldn't allow anyone else's judgment to affect what you choose to do. It's your life and your choice. So choose to do what's best for you," Kat told her.

"I will," Shanta assured. "Thanks for being here with me, Kat. Your support means a lot."

"I got you, boo. What are friends for?"

"It would be nice if Parker was here as well."

"Of course sis would be here no matter what if she could be. Despite our differences with her, Parker was a good friend to us. I still blame Castle for what happened to her," Kat said.

"You and I both," Shan agreed. If only she knew that Rob also played a part in Parker losing her life. She turned to Kat. "What choice do you think Parker would advise me make about the baby?"

"I can't say. I believe she would just advise you to make the choice your heart wants. And now is your chance to do so."

The nurse approached Shanta and collected her. Shan was led into the back of the clinic inside of a doctor's room by the nurse, where the procedure was to take place. Her mind was twisted and her stomach matched. The short, petite sister nurse took some blood samples and ran a few more tests that were protocol. And after the nurse determined that Shan was six weeks pregnant, she was a candidate for an abortion.

"The doctor will be in to see you shortly," the nurse informed before leaving Shanta to her thoughts.

What should I do? Shan contemplated. *Should I have the baby, or should I go through with the abortion?* She was left to make that choice on her own.

***

"What're you in here doin'?" Rich inquired as he stepped into the bedroom. He was smoking on a blunt of cookie weed.

"Just taking a look at some gowns for the wedding," Brittany answered while lying on her stomach in bed surfing the internet on her Apple laptop. "Ooh, babe! I like this one!"

"You can have whatever you like. Just don't show me the gown now 'cause I'd rather be amazed the day you come walkin' down the aisle in it."

"Aww. That's so sweet of you."

Rich sat on edge of the bed. "Only for you."

After the couple had made love all morning, they were in only their underwear. Rich wearing a pair of Ralph Lauren boxer-briefs and Brittany a black set of Victoria's Secret lingerie. It was barely afternoon and they planned to lounge around the house all day and just enjoy each other's company. They spent more time together subsequent to their vacay out in Cali because Rich realized just how much he wanted to be with Britt as much as possible. And with all of the beef in the streets Rich just needed to find some time to unwind.

"Me and your mom are going to plan the entire wedding together. She seems more excited about it than me," Brittany smiled.

"Good that she's excited for us. And she'll be even more excited whenever we have a baby," Rich mentioned.

Britt closed the laptop and then moved over to him. "Babe, I know Angie really wants grandkids, but I don't know if we're ready for kids."

Rich puffed the blunt. "Neither do I."

"Then let's just focus on each other for now."

"How 'bout I focus on you right now?" He placed the blunt in the ashtray on the nightstand.

"Boy, didn't you get enough this morning?"

"I can never get enough of you," Rich said as he pushed Britt back in bed then began planting kisses on her neck. His dick was hard and her pussy wet. He slid a hand down in between her legs.

The doorbell chimed, interrupting the moment. Neither of them was expecting any company.

"Stay put while I go and answer the door," Rich instructed her. He tossed on a pair of Nike jogger pants before leaving the bedroom. Once he opened the front door, he was surprised to see Shanta. "Shan, what're you doin' here?"

"I really need to talk to you," Shanta told him.

"A'ight. Come in." He allowed her inside and they took a seat on the couch in the front room. "Now what is it you need to talk to me about?"

Shan found it hard to speak. "Rich, I-I hope you don't look at me differently. But I want you to know that I... I was pregnant by Rob," she said in close to a whisper, not able to look him the eyes.

The news was like a punch to the gut for Rich. He didn't know how to feel or what to think in that moment. "Guess that's really why the talk of babies and all started to get to you durin' my ma's dinner, huh?" Rich scoffed and shook his damn head. "Shan, I'ont look at you any different. I'm sure it's already hard for you to look at yourself in the mirror. But I noticed that you said 'was'. Did you lose this baby too?"

"To be honest, I…I got an abortion."

"An abortion? When? Why?"

"I just got the procedure done today, right before coming here. And I chose to get an abortion because I just couldn't see myself having Rob's child, especially knowing that he's the reason why I had lost me and Don's unborn child. I love Don too much to do him like that. Also I wouldn't want to have you and Angie resent me. Besides, Rob never deserved to be with me in the first place," she expounded.

"Shan, it's unfortunate that you've lost two babies now 'cause neither one did anything to deserve that. But I do understand your choice. We both know that Don wouldn't care for you to have Rob's child. But do Rob know anything about the abortion?"

"No. He doesn't even know that I was pregnant. And as far as I'm concerned, I don't care to ever talk to him or see him again. I still can't believe that I fell for the one who had something to do with what happened to Don." Her tone displayed disappointment.

Rich rubbed her arm in solace and said, "Don't fault yourself. Don knows you wouldn't do somethin' like that to him on purpose. And trust, sooner or later, you won't have to worry about ever talkin' to or seein' Rob again whenever I catch him slippin'. You just try not to be so hard on yourself for any of this."

"I'll try."

Brittany came into the front room, now wearing a robe. "Babe, why didn't you tell me that Shanta was here? Hey girl."

"Hey to you too, Brittany," Shan replied.

"Can I get you anything?"

"That's okay. I was just about to leave anyway. Got Kat waiting for me in the car and I'm sure she's getting restless." Shanta stood. "By the way, I hope you two are enjoying engaged life. Be sure to send me an invite to the wedding."

"Fa sho'," Rich chimed in.

"Speaking of," Britt spoke up, "I was thinking that maybe you would like to be my bridesmaid."

Shanta gasped. "Yes, girl! I would love to be your bridesmaid!" She gave Britt a hug.

"Glad you'll be part of the weddin' ceremony, Shanta," Rich said.

"So am I. Well, I got to get going. Britt, if you need me for anything then just get in touch with me." Shanta made an exit.

"I didn't expect for her to come by," Brittany said as she locked the door behind Shan. She then moved over near Rich and stood before him.

"Me either." Rich pulled Brittany onto his lap. "It was nice of you to make Shan a bridesmaid."

"It's the least I can do after all she's been through. By the way, what did Shan want with you?"

"Believe it or not, she wanted to tell me that she was pregnant by Rob, but chose to get an abortion."

"Really?"

"Really. Said she didn't wanna have Rob's baby after losin' Don's the way she did."

"Well, I'm sure it had to be hard on her to choose to abort the baby."

"And she was concerned about me and my ma resentin' her if she chose to have the baby. I just hate that Shanta had to lose a second child due to that nigga, Rob. Sooner or later, I'ma make sure he'll never be a problem for me or mine again," Rich declared.

Brittany placed a hand on either side of his face and looked him in the eyes. "Rich, I know you already have a lot of things stressing you. So if you want to hold off on the wedding, then we can."

"Bae, I can't wait to have our weddin'. Just let me focus on the other things while you plan the ceremony."

"Alright. But either you going to be married to me or married to the streets. You can't have both."

Rich studied her a moment. "Don once told me that the streets love no one. So I rather have someone who love me." He kissed her sexy lips then laid her back on the couch. He opened her robe and began planting kisses on her body. "Now let's finish what we started before we was interrupted."

***

Kat and Shanta rode quietly in Kat's Jaguar. Glancing over at Shan, Kat could tell that her girl had a lot on her mind. And she just wanted to be supportive of her bestie.

"Girl, how're you doing after telling Rich about the abortion?" Kat cared to know.

"I'm fine. Just still learning to cope with the procedure," Shanta told her.

"It's going to take some time for you to fully cope with the abortion. I know the feeling. But remember that you made that choice because it's what's you thought was best," Kat went on to say.

"I know. And I remind myself of that," Shan responded.

"Does Rob even know anything about the abortion yet?"

"No, he doesn't."

"Are you going to tell him?"

"I... I don't know. On one hand I think he does need to know, but on the other hand, I feel he doesn't deserve to know at all." Shanta was conflicted about whether or not she should make Rob aware of her being pregnant with his child and choosing to abort it.

"Well, it's your choice of whether or not you tell Rob. Have you heard from him lately?"

Shan sighed. "Actually, he has tried calling, but I just can't bring myself to talk to him. Girl, I'm trying to find it in my heart to forgive him, but it's difficult. I will admit that at one point, I did love Rob, but learning that he had something to do with what happened to Don caused me to hate him."

"Shan, just don't let anyone or anything get you down," Kat said in support.

CHAPTER 14

It was late at night when Swindle pulled the Audi truck curbside in the hood. His truck made the first tracks in the new snow. He was there to check on one of his trap spots. Since Vito had gotten smoked, Swindle was left to take care of a lot of shit on his own. Even though he had gotten word that T-Mac was arrested for Vito's murder, Swindle knew there was still Rich and Danger he had to worry about. Plus, he couldn't forget that Bone had made him aware of Rob still being alive.

With niggas scheming to get at him, Swindle didn't like to be in the hood much at all unless it was absolutely necessary. And judging by the call he received from one of his pushers, Swindle figured it was necessary for him to go and make sure the spot was running accordingly. He stuffed his Glock in the pocket of his brown leather Prada coat before stepping out of the Audi truck. While clutching his pole, Swindle checked his surroundings with snow pelting down on him as he made his way towards the trap spot. He noticed the headlights of a vehicle coming up the street and was ready to draw his pole until the car continued down the street past him. Without bothering to knock, he entered the trap.

"What's so fuckin' important that you had to call me here?" Swindle asked in frustration as he stepped inside. He then immediately came upon Rob standing over his two pushers, who were lying face down on the floor dead.

"That depends on how important this is to you," Rob answered, training his FN on Swindle and using his free hand to hold Swindle's chain up for him to get a look at it.

Swindle knew better than to attempt to pull out his gun. "Why are you here, Rob?"

"I came here lookin' for you to get some info, but then I heard you was ducked off. And when I asked your boys here to tell me where you were, they swore that they didn't know shit. So I figure I'd have 'em bring you to me."

Swindle played it cool. "If you went through all that trouble to see me, then you must want some info pretty damn bad."

"As bad as you want this chain back."

"How 'bout you give me my chain and I'll let you keep your life?" He was gripping the pole inside of his pocket.

Rob scoffed. "Swindle, I'ma walk outta here with my life regardless. You can have your li'l chain back. Just tell me where to find Bone."

"How should I know?" Swindle feigned ignorance.

"We both know his ass came to you and sold you those bricks for the low. How else would you have these niggas pushin' weight for you? All I wanna know is where he is."

"Why do you wanna know where he is so damn bad?"

"'Cause he tried to kill me. And I won't let him get away with that. So, either you can tell me where he, is or I'll just burn you right here right now and then find Bone on my own," Rob forewarned.

Swindle thought on it a moment. He figured it was probably in his best interest to tell Rob where Bone was so he could send Rob into an ambush. "A'ight. I'll tell you where he is. He's layin' low at the Diamond Inn hotel. Said it's the last place you'd think to look for him. Now gimme my fuckin' chain and go."

"I never liked this damn chain anyway." Rob tossed the chain at Swindle's feet as he backed his way out the room before turning and hurrying out of the back door. He jumped into his Hellcat that was parked in the back alley then sped off with thoughts of getting revenge on Bone.

Swindle grabbed up his chain and put it on around his neck. He then tossed all of the money and drugs laying out inside of a pillowcase before exiting the trap and leaving the dead bodies behind. Now he had to warn Bone that Rob was on his way to the hotel. He figured that Bone could catch Rob off guard and then finish what he started. But if Rob was to kill Bone instead, then it was better Bone than himself is how Swindle felt. All in all, Swindle was looking out for himself, as usual.

While Swindle headed for his whip he pulled out his iPhone so he could call Bone to give him a heads up. As he reached Bone's stored number, he heard footsteps crunch in the snow over the sidewalk. Once he looked up he then noticed a nigga behind a gun vastly in approach. It was Danger.

Without any hesitation Swindle dropped his phone and drew his gun, then he and Danger exchanged shots. One of them had to die.

Blam, blam, blam, blam!

Boom, boom, boom!

During this exchange of gunshots, Danger struck Swindle with two bullets in the abdomen, which punctured one of lungs and pierced a kidney. Swindle collapsed onto the pavement, bleeding out and chasing his breath. As Danger walked up on him, Swindle regretted being caught slippin'. While riding through the hood, Danger had happened to spot Swindle on his way going inside of the trap and he had plotted to ambush him on the way out.

Danger stood over a helpless Swindle aiming the Draco down on his dome. "Thought you would get away."

In that moment, Swindle wished like hell everyone close to Don had been killed in order to save his own ass. "Nigga, go ahead and d-do what you g-gonna do," he dared him. "I-I think you—"

Boom, boom!

Without words, Danger pulled the trigger, blowing Swindle's final thoughts out, painting the snow crimson. Killing

Swindle was bittersweet for him because even though he had avenged Don and C-note, it still wasn't gonna bring them back. But he did feel a sense of vindication. And he was sure Rich would be satisfied with Swindle's bitch-ass having his brains blown out.

Danger turned for his whip. He jumped in and then skirted off down the street heading to see Rich with the news in person. Now that he had smoked Swindle, Danger knew that he was one less problem. But it wouldn't stop the money from bringing in more.

***

"How you holdin' up in there?"

"Like a real one."

The wipers swept back and forth, clearing the snow from the windshield while Rich babied the Lexus through traffic. He was on a collect call via Bluetooth with T-Mac, who was locked down in the Milwaukee County Jail. It bothered Rich that T-Mac was on lockdown and it made Rich want to do whatever he could to get him out of there sooner than later.

It had been two weeks since T-Mac was taken into custody for the murder of Vito and two others. There was video footage of Vito's murder outside of the restaurant, which led to T-Mac. Also his fingerprints were discovered on one of the spent shell casings found at the crime scene. Twelve tried hard pressing him about the identity of the second shooter that was with him, but T-Mac kept it solid and didn't speak about the body like a real one. Besides, he would rather take the hit because he wouldn't ever snitch on Danger or no one. Now all T-Mac could do is take the shit to trial with the lawyer Rich had retained for him. And T-Mac would rather be the suspect than the murder victim.

"T-Mac, you just keep holdin' up. The lawyer's gonna get you outta there," Rich encouraged.

T-Mac let out a sigh. "Listen Rich, no matter if I have to stay in here, I'ma keep holdin' up regardless. I just don't know if the lawyer will be able to get me outta here like you say."

"What do you mean?"

"I mean the lawyer tells me there's a lot of evidence stacked against me. And all I can do is take the shit to trial with the hopes of beatin' it like Rocky. If not, then I'll be facin' life in prison," T-Mac laid it out.

"Well, if there's anything I can do, then just let me know."

"Cuz, all I need you to do is stay alive in those streets. Part of me feel like I ain't out there to have your back. Especially with Swindle and Rob still around. But I know Danger has your back just as much as I would."

"Big facts. That's why Rob may still be around, but Swindle has left town for good." Rich offered him a tone of voice that told T-Mac exactly what he meant.

T-Mac snorted, then replied, "Guess the town wasn't big enough for the two of you. And I'm sure Rob will be leavin' town soon too."

"Soon as possible. Speakin' of Rob, can you believe Shanta told me that she was pregnant by the nigga?" he informed as he dipped the Lex' around a vehicle.

"I know Shan wasn't aware of who the nigga was before, but she can't have his seed."

"And she won't. Shan told me that she had gotten an abortion 'cause she couldn't stand the thought of havin' Rob's child after losin' Don's the way she did. I respect Shan's choice 'cause she did it to honor my big bro."

"And we both know that Don would turn over in his grave if she had Rob's seed."

"I know. Matter fact, it's been a while since I been to visit Don's grave, so I'll go there to ease my mind," Rich mentioned.

"Cuz, I know it's still hard on you after losin' your bro. But you still got me and Danger," T-Mac assured.

"And both of y'all got me. I'll never try to replace Don, but I'm just tryin' to be there for you all like he was. Especially for my mom."

"Listen, it's good that you wanna be there for your mom. It's what Don would want. She loves you as much as she loved him."

"And I'm glad that she's happy for me and Brittany. She's actually helpin' Britt with plannin' the weddin'."

"I never imagined you'd be the one to get married. But I'm happy for you, cuz."

"'Preciate it. But we gotta get you outta there 'cause I need you to be at the weddin' as my best man," Rich voiced.

"I mainly don't wanna miss the bachelor's party," T-Mac cracked. "But fa real, whether if I'm there or not, you know that I hope you nothin' but the best. So don't worry about me much."

The automated voice interrupted the phone conversation with a warning of there being one minute remaining on the call.

"Just know that I'm here for you, T-Mac," Rich guaranteed. "Look, I got shit to tend to in these streets so I'ma get goin'. Keep it solid."

"And while you in those streets, keep it close," T-Mac advised.

After the call ended, Rich was pushing his Lex through traffic with his thoughts drifting into the air as Lil Baby's tune "Humble" played at a moderate volume. He knew that T-Mac was holding strong because there was no other option. So Rich would be there for him no matter what. He had already lost

Don and C-note to the streets and he didn't want to lose T-Mac and Danger too. But he understood that the street lifestyle came with prison or death.

Rich pulled to a stop at a red light on MLK Drive. His thoughts shifted to Swindle and Vito no longer being a problem. But there was still Rob to deal with. He wanted to be absolutely sure that everyone who had anything to with what happened with him and his was put in the dirt. And part of him wanted to down Rob for getting Shanta pregnant when he was the reason why she lost Don's baby. But if he didn't find Rob soon then it would be too late before Rob skip town.

Then there was Brittany. Rich realized that she deserved for him to be committed to her as much as he was the streets. He loved Britt but the streets had made him, so he wasn't willing to choose one or the other. Rich needed Brittany to understand that if it wasn't for the streets then he wouldn't be the nigga she loved.

Once the light flipped green, Rich pulled off with traffic. He was clutching the pole in his lap while on his way. Rich knew it was in his best interest to take T-Mac's advice and keep it close while in the streets.

CHAPTER 15

In a room at the shabby Diamond Inn hotel, Bone set at the table loading his Tec-9 with plans to make his next move. On top of the table was the duffle bag that was filled with the majority of the money from the lick on Castle. He didn't go anywhere without his gun and the money close to him for safekeeping. As he slid a shell into the clip, he glanced over at the duffle bag and mused, *Only way anyone's taking mine is over my dead body.*

It had been a week since Bone had been laying low in the hotel. Just being there put him back into the mindset of the night of the caper on Castle which he, Max, TJ, and Rob had pulled off. However, Bone didn't feel any regret at all about his betrayal that night. If you asked him, they all owed him their lives for him taking the murder/robbery rap in the past any-fuckin'-way. At least that's how he validated his betrayal. But he knew Rob felt otherwise.

After a few days of hittin' Swindle's line only to get no response and not hearing anything back, quite frankly it started to bother Bone. While ducked off in the motel, Bone hadn't heard anything about Swindle being murdered. He just figured that Swindle was ignoring him purposely. Little did Bone know, Swindle got smoked right before he could call to warn him about Rob knowing where he could be found. Bone didn't know what to think, but he knew it was best that he think fast.

Done with laying low, Bone was preparing to go and take the money Rob had buried away and then find Rob and murk him. He no longer wanted to have to look over his shoulder for Rob. He wanted to finish what he had started. It was now or never; it was him or Rob. If only he knew that Rob was already onto him.

After Bone loaded up the Tec, he grabbed the duffle bag and made his way out of the room. On way down the hallway towards the staircase, he walked past the very room where he had left Rob n'em for dead. In that moment, he flashbacked to squeezing the trigger in Rob's face. He still couldn't believe that Rob managed to survive, and he regretted not making absolutely sure Rob was deceased. But this time around, Bone planned to stand over Rob and put a bullet in his fuckin' noggin to ensure he was dead and gone.

It was night out when Bone exited the hotel and snow fell lazily from the dark skies. He waltzed through the parking lot, headed towards his Yukon. Before Bone knew it, a Bentley SUV drew up before him and Sheik along with two shooters hopped out armed.

"Fuck you want?" Bone demanded while training his Tec on the trio.

"I want the money in the bag," Sheik told him with the two shooters flanking him leveling their guns.

"And nigga, who the fuck is you?"

"I'm the nigga who's here to take back the money that belongs to Castle."

Bone looked to be caught off-guard at the mention of Castle. He couldn't understand how they had found him. Instantly, he began regretting not killing Castle the night during the lick. He should have known that Castle would come gunning after whoever took his money.

Bone wasn't willing to give up the money without a war. After betraying his gang and nearly losing his life, there was no way anyone would just take the money back from him. Not Rob Castle. Unless it was over his dead body.

Prraat, prraat, prraat!

Blocka, blocka, blocka, blocka, blocka!

Without thinking twice about it, Bone opened fire on Sheik and the shooters. And instantly, Sheik returned fire along with the shooters. As bullets flew either way, Bone backpedaled in order to duck beside a parked vehicle while Sheik took cover behind the Bentley truck.

Both shooters tried advancing on Bone, who kept them back as he let off on them over the hood of the vehicle. One of the shooters was struck down from a deadly swarm of bullets to the torso. Once Bone attempted to dodge beside another parked SUV, the second shooter hit him in the leg, slowing Bone down.

Thinking fast as the shooter were about to advance on him, Bone dropped onto the snow-blanketed ground. Once he saw the shooter's feet, Bone aimed and then fired shots beneath the SUV, knocking the shooter off his feet with multiple shots. Then Bone finished him with more shots to the face.

Sheik slowly crept around the parked vehicles with his gun in the lead. He knew Bone wasn't willing to give up the money without dying. And Sheik had no problem with prying the duffle bag filled with the money from Bone's cold dead hands. As he rounded one of the vehicles, he noticed a trial of blood in the snow and proceeded to follow it.

Stepping over one of the dead shooters, Sheik followed the blood trail as he kept his eyes peeled for any sign of Bone. But none so far. Suddenly Sheik heard the ding from the door of a vehicle being opened. Then he turned and saw Bone about to jump into his Yukon.

With no hesitation, Sheik busted at Bone, who was quick to bust back. Sheik's Glock with the converted switch spat like a baby AK as slugs ripped through Bone. Gasping for air, Bone was halfway hanging out of the truck. His Tec was on the ground at his feet and the duffle bag was in the passenger seat. He had almost gotten away with his life and the money, but Sheik was there to take both.

Sheik walked up and reached over a helpless Bone then grabbed the duffle bag. He unzipped the duffle and looked inside at the numerous stacks of cash and so did Bone. Seeing all that money in the hands of his assailant made Bone resentfully think back to Rob telling him that just enough money will solve your problems and too much will kill you. Bone resented Rob now more than ever. If only he knew that it was actually Rob who had gone to Castle and told him where to find him as revenge.

Bone blinked away the resentful thought and found himself staring down Sheik behind the trigger.

Blocka!

After Sheik killed Bone, he headed for the Bentley and skirted off. Now that he had the money in his possession, Sheik was on his way to return it to Castle.

•••

While lying in bed at her place, Shanta was talking with Kat on her iPhone via FaceTime. It was late afternoon and Shan still wasn't up to get herself out of bed just yet. She was still in her pajamas with her hair wrapped in a silk scarf. Kat could tell that her bestie had been a bit down lately, so she wanted to do her all to uplift Shan as much as she could.

"You need to find a reason to be happy," Kat said.

"Maybe you should take your own advice. Because I can tell you been down ever since T-Mac been on lockdown. You must really like him," Shan replied.

"Is it that obvious? Well, I do like T-Mac a lot. He just seem to know how to handle me the right way. I miss him so much."

"Girl, if you really want him, then you should be there for him. T-Mac is a good nigga so he deserves a good bitch by his side."

"You're right," Kat concurred.

There was a knock at the front door. Shanta wasn't expecting any company, so she didn't know who it could be.

"Kat, let me call you back. There's someone at my door," Shan let her know as she slid out of bed.

"K. At least someone is able to get your ass out of bed," she chuckled.

"Whatevs! Smooches."

After the girls ended their call Shanta padded barefoot through the condo heading for the front door. Once she pulled opened the door then she was surprised to see Rob.

"You shouldn't be here," Shanta told him and went to slam the door shut in his face.

Rob prevented the door from shutting. "I'm only here because I have somethin' for you."

Shan scoffed. She stood with her arms folded and her weight shifted to one side. "Rob, I don't want anything you have to offer."

"Well, I think you really should have this." Rob came out of the pocket of his Balmain denim jeans with Don's Rolex. "Look, you may never forgive me, but at least know that what I felt for you was genuine. But apparently, I could never replace how you feel about Don. So here." He handed her the timepiece.

"Why give it back to me now?" she cared to know.

"I just thought that you should have it back as a memory. Especially since there's no way I can give you back Don or the baby you lost," he responded sincerely.

Just hearing him mention her losing not only Don but also the baby made Shan realize that he cared about her feelings more than she thought. "This means a lot to me," she told him.

"I thought it would. Shanta, I'm sure you don't really care to see me. But I just had to see you this one last time. You won't have to ever see me again because I'm leavin' town soon. I just hope that you can be happy no matter what." Rob turned to leave, but was stopped in his tracks when Shan grabbed his arm.

"Rob, there's something you should know before you go."

His brows furrowed and he curiously asked, "What is it?"

"I...I was pregnant with your child. But I chose to get an abortion," Shanta informed him reluctantly.

Rob snatched his arm from her grasp. "Shanta, why didn't you tell me that you were pregnant before? Instead you just chose to abort my baby without comin' to me first!" he spat angrily.

"I didn't find out that I was pregnant until after we broke up and I just couldn't bring myself to even talk with you about it. Because I was so hurt after learning that you had something to do with what happened to Don and me losing his baby. So I just felt like I couldn't have your baby," Shanta expressed.

Rob scoffed. "So part of you felt like you was gettin' even by abortin' my child since I'm the reason you had lost Don's unborn child unfortunately. Shanta, no matter what, my baby didn't deserve to be taken away for what I did," he snarled.

"And neither did Don's baby deserve to be taken away the way it was!" she cried. Tears wet her cheeks.

"You don't think I feel bad about what happened to you and his baby, Shan? Part of me wishes I could take that night back. But as fucked up as it may sound, if it would've never happened, then I wouldn't have ever had the opportunity of meetin' you. Maybe it would've been best if we never met. I thought it hurt badly when I lost you, but it hurts more to know that I lost a child."

"Rob——"

"No, Shanta," he intervened, cutting her off. "There's nothin' you can say to bring my child back, so I don't care to hear it. Just know that I'm glad this is the last time I'll be seeing you." Without further words, Rob turned on his way with Shanta watching his back as he walked away. He was hurt after learning that she chose to abort his unborn child, although he did understand her reason behind it. But that didn't mean Rob agreed with her choice.

Shanta closed the door then leaned back against it and slid down to the floor. She bawled into her palms. It hurt her that Rob seemed to care more about losing the baby more than herself. Now she began second guessing her choice to get an abortion. Then again, she felt the choice was best for her. But was it best for the child?

Through tear-filled eyes, Shan looked at the Rolex and instantly the sight of Don being murdered rushed into her mind. She also vividly remembered the sound of the gun cracking right before she was struck by the bullet that ultimately took Don's baby away. She shook away the horrific thoughts of that night. Shanta just wished that it was all a bad dream. But it was her reality. And holding the Rolex that once belonged to Don made it all too real.

CHAPTER 16

Rich was visiting his mom's place to check on her. It wasn't that he was concerned about her relapsing again. He just cared for her to know that he was there for her. And Angie appreciated that her son cared so much about her. It gave her more strength to remain sober because she didn't want to disappoint him again. They had grown closer than ever before since the passing of Don. It was what Don had always wanted for them.

Angie noticed that Rich didn't touch his bowl of mac & cheese she had cooked especially for him. She could read that something was on his mental. It wasn't that Rich didn't want to enjoy the food. He just didn't have much of an appetite. There was just so much on his mind with everything seeming to unfold vastly. If it wasn't one thing, then it was another.

They were in the kitchen of Angie's home. While she worked her way around the kitchen, Rich sat at the kitchen table. Both of them were used to Don usually being there, but that was a reality which no longer existed, so now all they had were each other.

"Baby," Angie began gingerly, "whatever is on your mind, you can tell Mama."

"How can you tell there's somethin' on my mind, Ma?" Rich asked, not realizing he had a tell.

Angie placed some dishes into the dishwasher. "Because you hadn't even taken a spoonful of your favorite food," she answered.

Rich glanced down at the still full bowl of triple cheese macaroni then back to his mom. "I guess you know me better than myself. It's just not the same eatin' your mac & cheese without Don. It was the one thing that could always bring me and him together. As much as we may have fought and disagreed, one thing for sure, we both enjoyed your mac & cheese equally."

"I can remember when you two were only kids and all we had to eat was macaroni and cheese many nights. But you two enjoyed it so much that it seemed like neither of you realized it was the only food I had available to cook for you. So I just started to cook it the best I could for you all because I wanted it to be the best meal I could feed the two of you."

"And it's always the best whenever I have it. Ma, I just been missin' Don so much lately," he told her.

"So have I." Angie moved over to the table and took herself a seat. "The good thing about missing him means we will never forget him," she consoled him.

"And I refuse to let anyone forget Don. Even if I gotta kill everyone who was involved in what happened to him just to keep Don's name alive." Rich pounded the table angrily.

Angie reached over the table and grabbed his hands in hers in solace. "Just know that killing anyone won't bring your brother back. But I do understand your anger."

"You're right, killin' anyone won't bring Don back. But at least it will be one less person to worry about. And the one person you no longer have to worry about is Swindle." Rich could see the relief in her eyes. He realized that Swindle had traumatized her by beating her and admitting to having Don murked. And frankly, Rich wanted him to be the dead more than anyone else due to what he had done to his mother and brother.

"Swindle deserved what he got. I'd rather he be dead than living the rest of his life in prison for the murder of Don," Angie said without remorse.

"Same here," Rich concurred. But what she had said made him think about the chance of T-Mac having to spend the rest of his life in prison. He leaned back in his seat and let out a breath. "Damn. Ma, I don't want T-Mac to have to do life in prison. I know if that's the case then he'll do his time like a real one. But I would hate for him to lose his life to the system due to his loyalty for me and Don."

"Look, T-Mac is my favorite nephew so of course I don't want anything bad to happen to him. However, you can't fault yourself because I'm sure he doesn't fault you. If need be, then you would be facing life in prison for your cousin, since you're loyal to him as well. All you can do is show him your loyalty by being there for him through this hard time," Angie expounded.

"Once again, you're right. I know T-Mac would do whatever for me and Don 'cause he's so loyal."

"And we both know that Don would be proud of him for that."

"Then I'm sure he'd also be proud of Shanta for her loyalty to him," Rich mentioned.

"What do you mean by that?"

"Ma, you should know that Shan ended up gettin' with one of the guys who had somethin' to do with what happened to Don. But she wasn't aware of who he was at first, and once she found out, then she immediately broke things off with him," he explained.

Angie couldn't fathom what she had just heard. "Rich, why didn't you tell me this before?"

"'Cause I didn't want you to worry about it with all that you had goin' on. But there's more. Shan told me that she was pregnant by the guy and had chosen to get an abortion 'cause she couldn't live with havin' his child when he was the reason she had lost Don's."

"But why didn't she tell me any of this on her own?"

"I'm sure she just found it hard to tell you 'cause she knows how much you want grandkids. She told me that she didn't want either of us to resent her."

"Well, she could have come to me. I'm sure it was hard on her to have to lose another baby like that. And I don't resent Shan because I know she will never do anything purposely to betray Don. She will always be my daughter in-law," Angie said.

"Maybe you should tell her that," Rich advised. "Speakin' of daughters in-law, Brittany told me that you'd be helpin' her with plannin' the weddin'. Just make sure she doesn't became a bridezilla." He chuckled.

"I'm happy that you have Brittany because she's good for you. So she deserves for you to always be there for her."

"And I will be. In fact, I should be there for Britt right now since she's home with a stomachache. I'll be sure to tell her that you send your love." Rich stood and offered his mom a hug before heading out on his way.

During Rich's commute to go and be with Brittany, he drove the Lexus real smooth over the slick street as light snow fell from the gray clouds. He bobbed his head to Lil Poppa's tune "Doing Better". While gripping the Glock in his lap, Rich was still paranoid because his brother had died with his gun. All he could think of was all of the bad days he had had and pray there would be better days. But he just had to wait on his time when it came.

The music cut off when a call came in on his iPhone. He answered via Bluetooth.

"What's up, Shanta?" Rich knew it was her by the display on his iPhone.

"Rich, I just thought you should know that I talked with Rob," Shanta informed him.

Rich braked at a stoplight. "When? Where?" he was eager to know.

"Yesterday. He had the nerve to show up here at my place."

"And what did he want with you?" Curious.

"Actually, he wanted to return me Don's Rolex. Said he thought I would want it."

Rich scoffed. "He can't give you back Don or the baby you lost due to him."

"Then I took the opportunity to tell him about the abortion. And even though he said that he understands my choice, he still took it hard."

"Now he knows how you feel. Look, if he happens to show up at your place again, then let me know so I can make sure you don't have to see him again."

"I don't think that will happen because he told me that he would be leaving town soon. And I don't care if I ever again see Rob. I couldn't live with having his child so I don't regret the abortion," she said frankly.

"Then he best leave town before I catch him, or the only place he'll be leavin' is this earth," Rich declared. "Speakin' of Rob and the abortion, I want you to know that I just told my ma about the entire situation. And she took it well. She knows how much your love and loyalty resides with Don."

"Well, I'm glad that you told her the entire situation because I just didn't know how she would take it. Rich, I love your mom dearly so I don't ever want her to resent me for any reason at all. Since I lost the baby, you two are the closest people I have to Don. And I can't forget about T-Mac."

"And trust, we want you close to us." He put on his blinker for a left-hand turn.

"Good to know." Shan was satisfied knowing how much Don's family embraced her. "By the way, how's T-Mac?"

Rich sighed. "Cuz is doin' all he can to hold up. But his situation is weighin' on him heavily. T-Mac's on lockdown due to his loyalty for me and Don, therefore I'll be loyal to him by bein' there for him."

"Luckily he has you there for him. Same goes for Brittany, she's lucky to have you."

"I'm the lucky one. And I look forward to makin' her my wife," Rich replied.

"Words of advice: happy wife, happy life," Shan half-joked.

"Good lookin' on the advice, sis," he chuckled. "If I'ont get home to her soon, then she won't be so happy with my ass."

Shanta thought about all of the times she worried about Don making it home to her safe and sound. "Rich just make it to her safely."

"No worries. My pistol off safety."

Once Rich ended the call, he couldn't help but to think about all of the wins and losses he had taken in the game thus far. He took his wins in stride and his losses as lessons. When the light flipped green Rich pulled off with traffic, watching his six in the rearview mirror for any signs of opps. Because one loss he wasn't willing to take was on his own life.

Arriving at his place, Rich decided that he would spin the block twice because he peeped what seemed to be a suspect vehicle tailing him. Better safe than sorry, he gripped tightly on his Glock. But once he turned the corner, the vehicle kept going straight, settling his suspicions. Rich parked once feeling comfortable that he wasn't being followed. After stepping out of the Lex' he chirped its alarm and made his way into the complex as he was showered by light snow.

After unlocking the front door, Rich then entered the condo. He shut the door behind himself then shrugged out of his Moncler coat and hung it up on the coat rack. Then he kicked off his snow-covered Timberlands boots at the door. Stepping through the apartment in search of Brittany, he found her in the bathroom standing before the mirror examining her own figure.

"What're you doin' in here?" Rich asked as he leaned up against the doorframe.

"Just checking myself out," Brittany answered. "Do I look like I gained some weight to you, babe?"

"Not that I can tell." He stepped up behind her and placed his hands on either side of her curvaceous hips. "But even if so, I'm in love with the shape of you."

"That's sweet! I'm just trying to be sure that I look my best in my wedding gown."

"Baby, you'll look your best after the weddin' when you take the gown off. Feel me?" He grinned.

Britt giggled. "Boy, your ass is so damn bad!"

"I know. Just don't tell my moms 'cause she thinks I'm too good for you," Rich said, just kidding.

"Don't worry, I won't tell her a thing. Matter fact, how's your mom?"

"She's good. I had a talk with her about a lot of shit. We mainly talked about family. I told her how much I've been missin' Don, and she encouraged me to always remember him no matter what. And I brought up feelin' at fault about T-Mac bein' on lockdown, then she told me I shouldn't feel that way 'cause he wouldn't want me to. Plus, I let her know all about Shanta's situation with the abortion, however she took it better than I thought and understood why Shan made her choice. And of course, I mentioned you, and she told me the best thing I can do is always be there for you."

"Sounds to me like your mom offered you a lot of great words."

"Yeah, she did. And so did Shan, who advised me to keep you happy if I want a happy life."

"I knew I liked Shanta for some reason." She smiled. "Well, I hope she's doing better now."

Rich perched himself back up against the sink. "Shan's still dealin' with everything that happened. Actually, she came face to face with the person who put her through the worst: Rob. And I could tell it bothered her."

"Did he hurt her? Is she okay?" Brittany cared to know.

"She's okay. But I can't believe that nigga had the fuckin' balls to show up at her place to give her back Don's Rolex, as if that's s'posed to make shit better." Rich scoffed.

"Now maybe she won't have to worry about seeing Rob again."

"Well, maybe so 'cause he told her that he'd be skippin' town soon. This town isn't big enough for the two us, so Rob best get outta town before I catch him," he declared. "I'm just glad that Shan chose to abort Rob's baby 'cause if it weren't for him, then she'd have Don's baby to carry on his legacy. And on top of that, my moms really wants grandkids and he took that away from her."

"It's sad because I know how much that child would have meant," Brittany said consolingly. She stepped close to him and grabbed his hand in hers then placed it on her tummy. "I'm just hoping that our child will mean just as much."

Rich's brows furrowed. "You're...pregnant?"

"Yes, baby!" she exclaimed. "I just found out today during my doctor's appointment. According to the doctor I'm three weeks along. Apparently I didn't have what I thought was a stomach ache after all."

"Bae, it means everything to me that you're carryin' my child. I'm glad that I'll be able to give my moms the grandchild she's always wanted. But what matters to me most is that I'm havin' a child with you," he expressed.

"It means so much for me to hear that. I love you, Rich."

"Love you too." Rich palmed her ass in both hands and pulled her close and began planting kisses on her neck.

"See, this is how I got pregnant in the first place," Britt half-joked.

"So let's see if we can make twins." Rich helped her out of her tight biker shorts, exposing her shaved pussy. He then sat her atop the sink, knelt between her agape legs, and placed his full lips on her twat. The wonderful feeling of him licking and suckling on her clit drove Brittany wild!

"Damn, babe, I love it when you eat me!" Britt moaned in pleasure. She palmed the back of his head and pressed his mouth onto her crotch while watching him work his lips and tongue on her. While Rich caressed her clit with his mouth, he also finger-fucked her pussy. "Ohhh, shit... I'm cuummmin, babe!"

Brittany's body racked with orgasm as she creamed all in Rich's mouth, and he licked and slurped up her cum. She pulled him onto his feet and kissed him deeply, and she tasted her own juices. She unfastened his Amiri jeans, then allowed them to fall down around his ankles. Pulling his hard dick out of his boxer-briefs, Brittany slipped it deep inside her wetness.

"Shit, girl. This pussy so fuckin' good," Rich groaned as he plunged his dick back and forth inside of her pussy walls. She dug her manicured nails into his back while taking the dick. It seemed the deeper he plunged in her, the wetter her pussy became. The sound of her moans of pleasure turned Rich on even more. He filled her with every inch of his hard-ness as he felt a nut build up in the tip of his cock. "Li'l baby, this wet got a nigga ready to bust!"

Rich stroked her rapidly until he busted a nut inside of her twat. He slumped forward on her, breathing heavily, and she wrapped her arms around his neck. The two really were in love with each other. And them having a child on the way made their love stronger.

Rich felt good to have her in his life, and he would do his all to keep her happy. Brittany was happy with him by her side, and she just wanted to make his life better. They were ready to be bonded 'til death do they part.

CHAPTER 17

The cell door was systematically opened, interrupting T-Mac while on his bunk bed reading *Blood On The Money* by J-Blunt. *Hell these flashlight cops want?* he wondered. He marked his book then left out of the cell to see what was up.

At the CO's booth, T-Mac was informed that he had a visitor. *Rich ain't s'posed to come 'til tomorrow so, who the hell could this be?* he pondered on his way towards the visitation booth. T-Mac entered the booth, and to his dismay, there on the monitor was Kat.

T-Mac took a seat in front of the monitor that Kat showed on. She smiled when she saw him on the monitor, and he smirked back at her. She noticed his body was tight and face was serious. However, he continued to hold his confident demeanor. Kat thought he had a way of looking good even wearing the county orange uniform that fit baggy on him.

"What are you doin' here?" T-Mac asked, conflicted about seeing her.

"Just thought I would come and see how you holding up in there," Kat answered.

"Kat, I 'preciate you comin' to see me but you don't have to."

"But I wanted to, T-Mac. So, how are you?"

"Long as I'm alive then I can't complain. You?"

"Life is good. Just been taking care of myself while trying to be there for Shanta."

"And how's she? I know she's been goin' through it since she lost Don."

"Losing Don has been the hardest thing on her. However, she's trying to cope with it. I guess the whole situation with Rob is what makes it harder on Shan."

"Shanta isn't at fault 'cause she wasn't aware of who the nigga was in the beginnin'. Besides, she won't have to worry about Rob sooner or later," he assured.

"Well, I'm sure she won't mind that after all he put her through physically, mentally, and emotionally. In case you don't know, Shanta was pregnant by Rob. But she chose to abort the baby on the strength of Don," she informed him.

T-Mac shook his head. "Damn. I hope she's fine. I commend her for making that choice 'cause I'm sure it was hard for her. How did Rich and Auntie Angie take the news?"

"Shan told me they took it better than she could expect."

"Shan's like family. Just 'cause Don isn't around doesn't change that much. As for all of the shit with Rob, he's gonna get his even if it takes for me to get out and give his ass what he got comin'. No cap." T-Mac had love for Shanta so he didn't feel any way towards her behind Rob. His issue was with Rob nonetheless.

"Rob deserves what he has coming," Kat concurred.

"But enough about that. Why'd you really come here today?" he wanted to know.

"Actually, there's something I need to talk with you about."

"Then let's talk."

Kat slightly exhaled. "Truth is, I can't stop thinking about you," she told him.

"Listen, I must admit that I've thought about you also. But we both know that it's nothin' serious between us."

"And I'm hoping that maybe we can change that. All you have to do is take a real chance."

T-Mac caressed his goatee. "Shorty, takin' real chances is what got me on lockdown fightin' for my freedom right now. And keepin' it real, I'ont know if I'll ever walk the streets a free man again. So I ain't got time to be stressin' about a bitch right now," he expounded.

"I understand your position. And I just want to be here for you as much as I can."

"Well, I'ont think that's a good idea."

"Really?" Kat said, feeling let down. Tears formed in her eyes.

It was tough for T-Mac to see her shed tears. He knew she was a bad bitch, so the fact that she cried made him understand how good of a bitch she was. On the low, he had feelings for her and wouldn't mind being with her, and obviously she held mutual feelings. Although T-Mac just didn't want to put her through the reality he was faced with.

T-Mac stood and said, "I'ont wanna put you through this. Take care of yourself. Now leave. And don't come back here again, Katherine." He walked out on her, even though he didn't want to.

Back in the confines of his cell, T-Mac lay on the bunk bed, staring at the graffiti-covered ceiling. After his talk with Kat, he thought about the possibility of him never going free. Kat made him understand just how much his freedom was important to others as well.

With his trial coming soon, T-Mac hoped that his lawyer would beat the case because he wanted to get back to the streets, but he realized that the odds were stacked against him. He would rather die in the streets than live the rest of his life in prison. Whichever, he was willing to accept his fate.

***

Needing to re-up, Rich had connected with Castle and they agreed to link up in order to do business. Thus far, business between them had gone accordingly. Their business proved to be lucrative for the both of them, so much so that this time around Rich had ordered eight bricks, and Castle was taxing him twenty-five Gs per key. However, Rich always came with the correct amount of money and Castle always made sure the weight was on point with the dope.

Walking through the Red Velvet strip club, Rich along with Danger were headed towards the VIP section to link up with Castle. It was the place Castle had chosen as the meeting grounds because he always felt most comfortable doing business in public places, especially since this would be the biggest business deal they would be making thus far. Plus, he was plugged with the owner, Diamond, so Castle knew he was secure there.

Being at this particular club was nostalgic for Rich. It brought back memories of the nights he and all of the others from his gang were there bringing life to the party. Then instantly he remembered that Don and C-note had lost their lives, and T-Mac was on lockdown fighting for his life. Now it was just him and Danger, and Rich couldn't help but wonder how life would eventually take either of them under.

Seated on the huge red velvet wraparound sofa in the VIP section, Castle along with Sheik popped bottles and enjoyed the club scene while awaiting Rich. Castle had grown to respect Rich as much as he did Don, because both of the brothers were all about money. And out of his respect, Castle wanted to let Rich know about Rob reaching out to him, because he wasn't playing both sides. Besides, though Castle had retrieved the money, he still wasn't willing to allow Rob to live.

Rich followed by Danger entered the VIP section, they greeted Castle and Sheik with daps before taking a seat on the sofa alongside them.

"Bottles on me," Castle offered, grabbing bottles of Ace of Spades from the bucket of ice on the table and handing them over.

"Gratitude. But before we pop bottles, we have some business to handle," Rich suggested.

"Then let's get down to business."

"Let's." Rich nodded his head at Danger, who carried along the Gucci backpack containing the re-up money and he sat it atop the table.

"Two-hunnit bands," Danger assured while Castle unzipped the backpack and eyed the stacks of cash.

"Sheik," Castle called and Sheik grabbed up the duffle bag from beside him and then slid it across the table.

"That's eight thangs," Sheik assured as Rich took a look inside of the bag at the wrapped keys.

Rich leaned back in his seat. "As always, it was nice doin' business with you. I'm just tryna get my money and weight up like Don would want me to."

"I feel you. And so far, I think Don would be proud of how far you came," replied Castle.

"Fa sho'." He popped the bottle of Ace then turned it up to his lips.

Castle shifted in his seat towards him. "Look, if we're gonna continue to do business, then outta respect, I want you to know that Rob had reached out to me. 'Cause I know how bad you got it out for that nigga behind what he did to Don."

"And why in the hell would Rob have any reason to reach out to you after he robbed you for your money?" Rich was confused.

"That's just it. He sent a random person to my place to let me know that if I wanted my money back then I should send someone to the Diamond Inn motel in order to retrieve it from a nigga named Bone. At first I thought it was a setup, but still I sent Sheik and his shooters to scope the place out," he explained.

"And just like Rob had said, there was the nigga Bone with the fuckin' money. I guess Rob wanted to make shit even," Sheik chimed in.

Danger scoffed. "If we kill ten of his niggas, it still won't be even," he added.

"Same here. So, Rob has another thing comin' if he thinks we even 'cause I got my money back," Castle input.

"I'ma get even when I bury Rob under dirt," Rich declared. He wasn't willing to let Rob walk the earth. Standing to his feet, he said, "We gotta make money moves so we'll get with y'all some other time." He headed for the exit with Danger in tow carrying the duffle bag.

In the club's parking lot, Rich and Danger stepped into the Range Rover. Danger slid behind the wheel and set the duffle bag on the backseat and as he went to start the ride he noticed Rich resting his head back against the headrest of the passenger seat. It was apparent to him that something was on Rich's mindset. They set there a moment just watching the snow fall.

"What's on your mind, Rich?" Danger inquired.

Rich took a breath. "Just the shit that's been goin' on. Can't believe that nigga, Rob, sent word to Castle," he said heatedly. Danger shifted towards him. "You think Castle knows more than he's tellin' us?"

"Naw. Castle ain't the type of nigga to let anyone try him and get away with it. What I think is Rob's just tyin' up loose ends. So I wouldn't be surprised if he has it in mind to come for us when we least expect it."

"Look, don't trip. We'll smoke Rob just like we did Swindle and Vito," Danger insisted.

"We just gotta be sure to slide on his ass without it leadin' back to us. Just look at what happened with T-Mac," Rich mentioned.

"It's fucked up that T-Mac's on lockdown for a body. Good thing he's a solid nigga or he could easily snitch me out."

"Cuz will never snitch. Besides, the lawyer I retained for him is one of the best in the game at beatin' bodies."

"Then let's hope he beats the body, 'cause we need T-Mac in these streets," Danger said. He respected that Rich and T-Mac were down to get even just as much as he is. "Don and C-note were my closest niggas. It's crazy how you and T-Mac remind me of them. And I'm sure they respect that y'all down to avenge their murders."

"Don and C-note mean so much to me and T-Mac, so we'll ride or die for them niggas. And trust, we feel the same about you."

"And I trust you niggas with my life," Danger told him.

"Same here," Rich assured. "Now let's get outta here so we can get to the money."

Martell "Troublesome" Bolden

CHAPTER 18

The bridal boutique was preoccupied with brides-to-be, and Brittany was one of them. She was there to pick out her brides-maids dresses and had asked along Angie and Shanta. Since they would be part of the wedding ceremony Brittany thought it was a good idea to have them help her.

"I wonder what's keeping Shanta," Britt said as she looked over the array of dresses.

"Shan is reliable, so she'll be here soon," Angie assured. "Listen, Brittany, I want to thank you for asking me to help with planning the wedding. It means a lot to me."

"And it means a lot to me that you care to help, Angie."

"From now on, call me Mom since you're going to be my daughter-in-law. And I'm glad that my son will be marrying you because you're good for him."

"Rich is good for me as well, so I'm glad he I'll be marrying him too," Britt told her. She ceased looking over dresses and peered at Angie. "Ang——Mom, I'm glad that you're happy for me and Rich."

Angie placed a hand on her arm in comfort. "What matters most is that you and Rich are happy together."

"And we are," Britt reassured. She noticed Shanta followed by Kat enter the boutique. "Oh, there's Shan now."

"Told you she'll be here. But I didn't expect for her to bring along Kat," Angie commented.

"Neither did I." Brittany still felt a way about how Kat disrespected her by coming onto her man right in front of her. Of course she knew that Kat could never take Rich from her no matter what. But for her to even flirt with that thought made Britt uncomfortable.

Shanta approached and offered Brittany and Angie hugs. "Sorry I'm late, but I had to swing by and pick up Kat. Hope you don't mind that I brought her along."

"No girl, I don't, as long as she don't mind being here," Britt responded, keeping it classy.

"Yes, I want to be here to support you," Kat chimed in. "I never got the chance to congratulate you on your engagement so congrats, girl. I'm sure you're going to be the best wife Rich could ask for."

"Thanks, girl."

"Look, Brittany, I apologize for how things started out between us. I hope we can patch things up and perhaps become homegirls." Kat felt it necessary to apologize for her past behavior towards Brittany because she realized just how unfair she had been.

"It's nice of you to apologize, Kat. And if you're going to be one of my homegirls, then you also have to be one of my bridesmaids!" Brittany exclaimed.

"Sounds good!" Kat responded.

"It's good to see you two getting along because we girls need to lift each other up," Angie commented.

"God knows I can use all of the uplifting that I can get since the abortion," Shanta mentioned.

Angie draped an arm around her shoulder and said, "Girl, we're here for you. By the way, how are you doing since the procedure?"

"Well, I'm still processing it. Although I do feel like it was the right choice for me because I just couldn't have that child after losing Don's the way I did."

"I'm sorry that you had to go through that, Shan. But you made the best choice for you," Brittany added. In that moment, she thought to tell them about her being with child. She just hoped that everyone took it well, especially Shan since she had just lost her second child recently. "Listen, I hope this isn't too soon, but I want you all to know that me and Rich will be having a baby."

Angie gasped and gently rubbed Brittany's tummy. "Oh, my goodness! Knowing that I'm going to be a grandma makes me so proud."

"I was hoping it would."

"I guess I should congratulate you for a second time to-day," Kat said with a smile.

Shanta grabbed Brittany's hands in hers. "Brittany, I'm happy for you and Rich. And I'm sure that you're going to be a wonderful mom."

"Thanks. I know it's been tough on you after losing two babies, so it means a lot to me that you're happy for us. I can only hope to be as wonderful of a mom as I'm quite sure you would be," Brittany said sincerely. She looked to all of the girls. "I'm grateful that all of you are here for me, and are happy for me and Rich."

"I think I speak for all of us when I say we just want the best life for you and Rich," Angie responded.

"And hopefully he and I will be together for the rest of life," Britt added. "Now, let's go and look for some brides-maids dresses that'll have you girls looking as gorgeous as the bride."

It meant a lot to Brittany that everyone was happy that she and Rich would be bounded together in holy matrimony. And with the baby on the way, she just wanted for her life with him to be perfect. But she knew the reality of being with a nigga who lived the street life was far from some love story with a fairytale ending. Britt had no doubt that Rich wanted marriage with her, although she was aware that he was already married to the streets most likely 'til death do him part.

Martell "Troublesome" Bolden

CHAPTER 19

Rob pulled his Hellcat to stop in the graveyard. He was there for his money in the grave. He placed the FN 5.6 equipped with a thirty-two-shot stick on his person before grabbing the shovel from the backseat, then he stepped out. Slogging his way through the snow that blanketed the ground, he unknowingly walked past Don's tombstone while on his way towards where he had buried his money. Usually, Rob would come to the burial grounds in order to deposit more money into the stash, but instead, he was there to withdraw all of the blood money out of it.

For the past few years, subsequent to each caper, he had stashed away money in the grave with a goal in mind. His goal was a million dollars and then he would get out of the stickup game for good. And had it not been for him being betrayed over the money from the biggest caper that he and the others had pulled off, then Rob would have met his goal undoubtedly. After he was to dig up the money, then as planned, he would get the hell out of town, far away from the droves of beefs, hail of bullets, and spilling of blood.

As Rob plunged the shovel into the earth and began digging up the snowy soil, he couldn't help but to think back to all of the beefs he had been faced with during his years of gettin' it the ski mask way. There were several times when he nearly lost his life trying to get rich. However, he had managed to evade death thus far. But he couldn't say the same about his deceased niggas. TJ had always been close to him; Max was always down for him; and Bone was once loyal to him. Rob hated to lose each of them the ways he did, because no matter what they had been through, he loved them to death. After all that Rob had been faced with, he was ready to take off the ski mask once and for all.

Once Rob dug deep enough, the shovel made a thud against the wooden box in the soil. He used his hands to dig out the rest of the dirt from atop the box, and once he pulled it out of the ground, he then opened its lid and revealed numerous stacks of cash. There was over seven hundred grand in the box. Though he didn't meet his goal of stashing a million dollars away, he knew that he had just enough money there to change his life. And tonight, he would be taking the money with him then leaving town and the stickup game for good.

**

Rich turned his Lexus into the graveyard. He was on his way to visit Don's gravesite. It had been some time since he was last there, and he felt the need to go alone and visit because he was missing Don a lot. While Lil Durk's tune "Death Ain't Easy" played at a modest volume in the background, Rich gripped the Glock .45 equipped with a thirty-two-shot stick in his lap and reminisced about the deaths of Don and the others.

Rich took it hard when his brother was murked and was still trying to cope with it. And the loss of C-note was also hard on him because C-note was very close to Don. The only way Rich could feel better about their deaths is if he get revenge. His mind shifted to T-Mac and Danger, who were both willing to take out revenge for their niggas by any means necessary. He knew that Danger was determined to avenge the deaths of Don and C-note, even if it meant going out with his finger on the trigger. And T-Mac undoubtedly wanted to get even, no matter if it came with him having to be in prison for the rest of his natural life. Rich had witnessed all of his niggas shed blood, sweat, and tears in the streets, and he understood that the street life came with prison or death.

However, Rich wanted to keep from going to prison for life or meeting an early death himself. Therefore, he knew that he would have to be vigilant. Because now he had more to live for with having Brittany in his life and their baby on the way. He looked forward to being a husband to Britt and a father to their unborn child, and he would do anything to be there for his family. Not to mention he knew that Don would want him to be there for Angie and Shanta. No matter the past relationship Rich had had with Angie, he loved her and understood why Don always reminded him that they only get one mother. As for Shan, Rich would always be close to her because he knew that she had meant so much to Don. Much like his big brother, Rich just wanted to provide for him and his in the streets.

After Rich bossed up following Don's death, he quickly learned that the only rule in the streets was survival of the fittest. And Rich realized that with everyone vying for money, power, and respect in the streets many wouldn't survive, and his brother being murked had proved that to be a fact. Yet it didn't prevent Rich from trying to take over the streets by any means in Don's wake.

***

The graveyard was scarce on this cold evening. The cemetery's oak trees branches bowed low from the weight of snow, and snow covered the ground. With daylight turning into nightfall the skies was growing dark, giving the place an eerie presence as snow blew around in the heavy wind and piled against tombstones. There seemed to be countless tombstones protruding from the ground. Many looked as though the gravesites hadn't been attended for quite a while. Being in the graveyard had its way of reminding one that there was no way to evade death.

As Rich pulled his Lex to a stop near Don's gravesite, he saw the Hellcat parked there and instantly knew it belonged to Don's killer, Rob. Without thinking twice, Rich jumped out of the car and hurried towards Rob with his gun in hand. Overhearing footsteps in the snow caused Rob to look back over his shoulder, and immediately, he noticed there was Don's brother, Rich! Without hesitation, he spun on his heels and whipped his gun out. The two stood some length apart while holding one another at gunpoint, Rich standing near his brother's tombstone and Rob standing near his box of blood money.

"Why the hell are you here?" Rich demanded.

"No, why the hell are *you* here?" Rob retorted demandingly.

"I'm here to visit my brotha's grave."

"And I'm here to collect my money in the grave."

Simultaneously, Rich glanced down at the shovel and realized it had been used to dig up the box of money. Rob glanced down at the tombstone and realized it actually belonged to Don. It was ironic that they had found each other in the graveyard of all places after looking for each other in the wake of Don's death. The enemies locked glares, Rich's eyes displaying no mercy and Rob's eyes revealing no remorse. Both had their fingers on the triggers and their minds on murder.

"Been lookin' for you ever since I found out that you murked Don," Rich told him sternly.

"And I been lookin' for you ever since findin' out that because of Don, you wanted me dead," Rob replied in a matter-of-fact tone.

"I can't let you get away with takin' my brotha's life. Then you had some fuckin' nerve to get with the love of his life, Shanta. Just know that she hates you as much I do."

"Me takin' your brotha out is just part of the street lifestyle. As for Shanta, I can understand why he loved her 'cause so did I. But she gave me reason to hate her too when her ass chose to abort my child like it was nothin'."

"Nigga, Shan had good reason to choose to get an abortion, since it's because of you that she lost Don's unborn child in the first damn place!" Rich raved. He was consumed with anger.

"Look, I'm just here to take my money and leave town, then you and Shan won't have to ever see me again."

"Rob, you've already taken a lot from us when you took my brotha. So, the last thing I'ma do is let you take that money."

"Over my dead body will you stop me from takin' this money and leavin'."

"Then in order to stop you, I'll kill you dead. That's on my brotha's grave," Rich swore, staring him dead in the eyes.

Rob scoffed and then hissed, "Your brotha must be turnin' over in his grave right now knowin' that you're 'bout to die by the same gun that he did."

Boom, boom, boom, boom!

Boc, boc, boc, boc, boc, boc!

The two matched guns. Rich's Glock converter had a switch which made it shoot rapidly, and Rob's FN shot the same. As rapid gunfire was exchange both of them took cover. Rich crouched behind a random erect tombstone while Rob slunk beside the large oak tree. Some of the bullets chipped away at the tombstone and some knocked chunks from the tree.

Rich squeezed his trigger with motive to kill. His motive was to get revenge for Don. He couldn't let Rob live and take the money then skip town. It's kill or be killed, he contemplated.

Rob pulled his trigger with no intent to die. His intention was to do Rich just like he had done Don. He wouldn't let Rich live to stop him from taking the money then leaving town. *It's do or die*, he mused.

Boc, boc, boc, boc, boc, boc!

Boom, boom, boom, boom!

The exchange of gunfire kept them both pinned in their perspective places. Both were seeking for a clean shot while trying not to take a bullet themselves during the gunfight. Bullets whizzed by Rich just missing his head and some narrowly missed Rob grazing the right side of his torso. However, thus far they evaded death.

Taking his chances, Rob stepped from beside the tree while dumpin' at Rich and keeping him pinned down. He grabbed the box of cash by its handle and began dragging it through the snow towards his car. Not willing to chance him getting away, Rich rose from behind the tombstone, then busted at Rob and slowed him down.

Rich popped Rob in the leg, causing him to drop the box and stumble. Rob instantly turned and then clapped back and popped Rich twice, once in the shoulder and the second in the arm. However, both were still standing, slugging back and forth, like Ali versus Frazier. And it was inevitable that one of them would go down for the count.

Simultaneously, the two let off rapid gunfire at one another. Rob took a bullet in the shoulder while Rich took two to the chest. The shots caused Rich to flail backwards and fall into Don's tombstone. Seizing the chance, Rob hobbled along and stood over him. Rich looked up at him helpless as his breath plumed into the cold air while he fought to breathe and blood wept from his bullet wounds.

"Now your brotha is the reason you'll die, Rich," Rob hissed.

"At...l-least if I...die for my b-brotha then...I-I won't d-die in vain," Rich managed to retort. He mustered enough strength to faintly grab for his gun in the snow beside him. But Rob targeted his chest and riddled it with bullets.

Boom! Boom! Boom!

Blood splattered onto the tombstone and lots of it stained the snow crimson as Rich bled profusely.

Rob grabbed up the box of money and made his way to the Hellcat. As he slid behind the steering wheel, he tossed the box into the passenger seat. And now that he had collected his money, he would be able to go through with his plans to retire someplace far away and permanently be out of the stick-up game.

Bringing the engine to life, Rob sped off and departed the graveyard, leaving Rich bleeding to death just as he once did Don. He had given some bullets and he had taken some bullets, but he had managed to outlive his comrades and enemies.

Rich lived just long enough to see his life flash before his eyes. He flashbacked to his moms cooking her specialty mac and cheese; to when he and Don were just kids with little worries; to seeing how beautiful Brittany was the very first time; to the proud moment of learning about his unborn child... And now he was about to die by the gun of the same nigga who murked his brother.

In that moment, Rich drew enough strength to fingerpaint "ROB" on Don's tombstone in his own blood so that his and Don's murders both would be avenged. Rich wanted it to be known who had murdered him before losing his soul.

Martell "Troublesome" Bolden

EPILOGUE

The murder of Rich was just as devastating as Don's for everyone. And since Rich had literally died on his brother's grave, it proved just how much he had been willing to do or die for Don. It was no secret who had murdered Rich once his corpse was discovered beside Don's tombstone with "ROB" written on it in his own blood.

Angie was heartbroken that she had lost both of her sons, although she was grateful that they were reunited in spirit. On the strength of them, she would remain clean and sober.

Brittany had lost the love of her life but gave birth to his baby boy that was the spitting image of Rich, who she had named after him. She vowed to raise her son to know all about his late father and his uncle.

Shanta still hadn't fully gotten over the loss of Don and their unborn child and losing Rich by the gun of Rob caused her to feel guilty. However, she still was there for Angie because she knew it's what Don and Rich would want of her.

T-Mac had taken his murder case to trial and was subsequently found guilty, which resulted in him being sentenced to life in prison, although he was working on an appeal with the intent of having his case overturned. And if ever he regained his freedom, then he swore to avenge Don and Rich's murders by personally killing Rob.

As for Rob, after all that he had been through, he just wanted to live without having to worry about any payback. However, he figured that murdering Don and Rich could possibly come with a price to pay. So he had made himself a new life in New York with the money he had had buried away.

Once Rich had been laid to rest in his grave, he was buried beside Don. In fact, the gravesite was located where Rob had once buried his money in the grave...

The End…

Lock Down Publications and Ca$h Presents assisted publishing packages.

BASIC PACKAGE $499
Editing
Cover Design
Formatting

UPGRADED PACKAGE $800
Typing
Editing
Cover Design
Formatting

ADVANCE PACKAGE $1,200
Typing
Editing
Cover Design
Formatting
Copyright registration
Proofreading
Upload book to Amazon

LDP SUPREME PACKAGE $1,500
Typing
Editing
Cover Design
Formatting
Copyright registration
Proofreading
Set up Amazon account

Upload book to Amazon
Advertise on LDP Amazon and Facebook page

***Other services available upon request. Additional charges may apply
Lock Down Publications
P.O. Box 944
Stockbridge, GA 30281-9998
Phone # 470 303-9761

Submission Guideline

Submit the first three chapters of your completed manuscript to ldpsubmissions@gmail.com, subject line: Your book's title. The manuscript must be in a .doc file and sent as an attachment. Document should be in Times New Roman, double spaced and in size 12 font. Also, provide your synopsis and full contact information. If sending multiple submissions, they must each be in a separate email.

Have a story but no way to send it electronically? You can still submit to LDP/Ca$h Presents. Send in the first three chapters, written or typed, of your completed manuscript to:

LDP: Submissions Dept
Po Box 944
Stockbridge, Ga 30281

DO NOT send original manuscript. Must be a duplicate.

Provide your synopsis and a cover letter containing your full contact information.

Thanks for considering LDP and Ca$h Presents.

NEW RELEASES

TOE TAGZ 4 by AH'MILLION
A GANGSTA'S QUR'AN 4 by ROMELL TUKES
THE COCAINE PRINCESS 2 by KING RIO
SAVAGE STORMS 3 by MEESHA
LOYAL TO THE SOIL 3 by JIBRIL WILLIAMS
THE STREETS WILL NEVER CLOSE by K'AJJI
MONEY IN THE GRAVE 3 by MARTELL "TROUBLE-SOME" BOLDEN

BLOOD OF A BOSS **VI**

SHADOWS OF THE GAME II

TRAP BASTARD II

By **Askari**

LOYAL TO THE GAME **IV**

By **T.J. & Jelissa**

IF TRUE SAVAGE **VIII**

MIDNIGHT CARTEL IV

DOPE BOY MAGIC IV

CITY OF KINGZ III

NIGHTMARE ON SILENT AVE II

THE PLUG OF LIL MEXICO II

By **Chris Green**

BLAST FOR ME **III**

A SAVAGE DOPEBOY III

CUTTHROAT MAFIA III

DUFFLE BAG CARTEL VII

HEARTLESS GOON VI

By **Ghost**

A HUSTLER'S DECEIT III

KILL ZONE II

BAE BELONGS TO ME III

By **Aryanna**

KING OF THE TRAP III

By **T.J. Edwards**

GORILLAZ IN THE BAY V

3X KRAZY III

STRAIGHT BEAST MODE II

De'Kari

KINGPIN KILLAZ IV

STREET KINGS III

PAID IN BLOOD III

CARTEL KILLAZ IV

DOPE GODS III

Hood Rich

SINS OF A HUSTLA II

ASAD

RICH $AVAGE II

By Martell Troublesome Bolden

YAYO V

Bred In The Game 2

S. Allen

CREAM III

By Yolanda Moore

SON OF A DOPE FIEND III

HEAVEN GOT A GHETTO II

By Renta

LOYALTY AIN'T PROMISED III

By Keith Williams

I'M NOTHING WITHOUT HIS LOVE II

SINS OF A THUG II

TO THE THUG I LOVED BEFORE II

IN A HUSTLER I TRUST II

By Monet Dragun

QUIET MONEY IV

EXTENDED CLIP III

THUG LIFE IV

By **Trai'Quan**

THE STREETS MADE ME IV

By **Larry D. Wright**

IF YOU CROSS ME ONCE II

By **Anthony Fields**

THE STREETS WILL NEVER CLOSE III

By K'ajji

HARD AND RUTHLESS III

THE BILLIONAIRE BENTLEYS III

Von Diesel

KILLA KOUNTY III

By Khufu

MONEY GAME III

By Smoove Dolla

JACK BOYS VS DOPE BOYS II

A GANGSTA'S QUR'AN V

By Romell Tukes

MURDA WAS THE CASE II

Elijah R. Freeman

THE STREETS NEVER LET GO II

By Robert Baptiste

AN UNFORESEEN LOVE III

By **Meesha**

KING OF THE TRENCHES III
by **GHOST & TRANAY ADAMS**

MONEY MAFIA II

LOYAL TO THE SOIL III

By **Jibril Williams**

QUEEN OF THE ZOO II

By **Black Migo**

THE BRICK MAN IV

THE COCAINE PRINCESS III

By King Rio

VICIOUS LOYALTY II

By Kingpen

A GANGSTA'S PAIN II

By J-Blunt

CONFESSIONS OF A JACKBOY III

By Nicholas Lock

GRIMEY WAYS II

By Ray Vinci

KING KILLA II

By Vincent "Vitto" Holloway

Available Now

RESTRAINING ORDER **I & II**

By **CA$H & Coffee**

LOVE KNOWS NO BOUNDARIES **I II & III**

By **Coffee**

RAISED AS A GOON I, II, III & IV

BRED BY THE SLUMS I, II, III

BLAST FOR ME I & II

ROTTEN TO THE CORE I II III

A BRONX TALE I, II, III

DUFFLE BAG CARTEL I II III IV V VI

HEARTLESS GOON I II III IV V

A SAVAGE DOPEBOY I II

DRUG LORDS I II III

CUTTHROAT MAFIA I II

KING OF THE TRENCHES

By **Ghost**

LAY IT DOWN **I & II**

LAST OF A DYING BREED I II

BLOOD STAINS OF A SHOTTA I & II III

By **Jamaica**

LOYAL TO THE GAME I II III

LIFE OF SIN I, II III

By **TJ & Jelissa**

BLOODY COMMAS I & II

SKI MASK CARTEL I II & III

KING OF NEW YORK I II,III IV V

RISE TO POWER I II III

COKE KINGS I II III IV V

BORN HEARTLESS I II III IV

KING OF THE TRAP I II

By **T.J. Edwards**

IF LOVING HIM IS WRONG…I & II

LOVE ME EVEN WHEN IT HURTS I II III

By **Jelissa**

WHEN THE STREETS CLAP BACK I & II III

THE HEART OF A SAVAGE I II III

MONEY MAFIA

LOYAL TO THE SOIL I II

By **Jibril Williams**

A DISTINGUISHED THUG STOLE MY HEART I II & III

LOVE SHOULDN'T HURT I II III IV

RENEGADE BOYS I II III IV

PAID IN KARMA I II III

SAVAGE STORMS I II III

AN UNFORESEEN LOVE I II

By **Meesha**

A GANGSTER'S CODE I &, II III

A GANGSTER'S SYN I II III

THE SAVAGE LIFE I II III

CHAINED TO THE STREETS I II III

BLOOD ON THE MONEY I II III

A GANGSTA'S PAIN

By J-Blunt

PUSH IT TO THE LIMIT

By **Bre' Hayes**

BLOOD OF A BOSS **I, II, III, IV, V**

SHADOWS OF THE GAME

TRAP BASTARD

By **Askari**

THE STREETS BLEED MURDER **I, II & III**

THE HEART OF A GANGSTA I II& III

By **Jerry Jackson**

CUM FOR ME I II III IV V VI VII VIII

An **LDP Erotica Collaboration**

BRIDE OF A HUSTLA **I II & II**

THE FETTI GIRLS **I, II& III**

CORRUPTED BY A GANGSTA I, II III, IV

BLINDED BY HIS LOVE

THE PRICE YOU PAY FOR LOVE I, II ,III

DOPE GIRL MAGIC I II III

By **Destiny Skai**

WHEN A GOOD GIRL GOES BAD

By **Adrienne**

THE COST OF LOYALTY I II III

By Kweli

A GANGSTER'S REVENGE **I II III & IV**

THE BOSS MAN'S DAUGHTERS I II III IV V

A SAVAGE LOVE **I & II**

BAE BELONGS TO ME I II

A HUSTLER'S DECEIT I, II, III

WHAT BAD BITCHES DO I, II, III

SOUL OF A MONSTER I II III

KILL ZONE

A DOPE BOY'S QUEEN I II III

By **Aryanna**

A KINGPIN'S AMBITON

A KINGPIN'S AMBITION **II**

I MURDER FOR THE DOUGH

By **Ambitious**

TRUE SAVAGE I II III IV V VI VII

DOPE BOY MAGIC I, II, III

MIDNIGHT CARTEL I II III

CITY OF KINGZ I II

NIGHTMARE ON SILENT AVE

THE PLUG OF LIL MEXICO II

By **Chris Green**

A DOPEBOY'S PRAYER

By **Eddie "Wolf" Lee**

THE KING CARTEL **I, II & III**

By **Frank Gresham**

THESE NIGGAS AIN'T LOYAL **I, II & III**

By **Nikki Tee**

GANGSTA SHYT **I II &III**

By **CATO**

THE ULTIMATE BETRAYAL

By **Phoenix**

BOSS'N UP **I , II & III**

By **Royal Nicole**

I LOVE YOU TO DEATH

By **Destiny J**

I RIDE FOR MY HITTA

I STILL RIDE FOR MY HITTA

By **Misty Holt**

LOVE & CHASIN' PAPER

By **Qay Crockett**

TO DIE IN VAIN

SINS OF A HUSTLA

By **ASAD**

BROOKLYN HUSTLAZ

By **Boogsy Morina**

BROOKLYN ON LOCK I & II

By **Sonovia**

GANGSTA CITY

By **Teddy Duke**

A DRUG KING AND HIS DIAMOND I & II III

A DOPEMAN'S RICHES

HER MAN, MINE'S TOO I, II

CASH MONEY HO'S

THE WIFEY I USED TO BE I II

By Nicole Goosby

TRAPHOUSE KING **I II & III**

KINGPIN KILLAZ I II III

STREET KINGS I II

PAID IN BLOOD **I II**

CARTEL KILLAZ I II III

DOPE GODS I II

By **Hood Rich**

LIPSTICK KILLAH **I, II, III**

CRIME OF PASSION I II & III

FRIEND OR FOE I II III

By **Mimi**

STEADY MOBBN' **I, II, III**

THE STREETS STAINED MY SOUL I II III

By **Marcellus Allen**

WHO SHOT YA **I, II, III**

SON OF A DOPE FIEND I II

HEAVEN GOT A GHETTO

Renta

GORILLAZ IN THE BAY **I II III IV**

TEARS OF A GANGSTA I II

3X KRAZY I II

STRAIGHT BEAST MODE

DE'KARI

TRIGGADALE I II III

MURDAROBER WAS THE CASE

Elijah R. Freeman

GOD BLESS THE TRAPPERS I, II, III

THESE SCANDALOUS STREETS I, II, III

FEAR MY GANGSTA I, II, III IV, V

THESE STREETS DON'T LOVE NOBODY I, II
BURY ME A G I, II, III, IV, V
A GANGSTA'S EMPIRE I, II, III, IV
THE DOPEMAN'S BODYGAURD I II
THE REALEST KILLAZ I II III
THE LAST OF THE OGS I II III
Tranay Adams
THE STREETS ARE CALLING
Duquie Wilson
MARRIED TO A BOSS I II III
By Destiny Skai & Chris Green
KINGZ OF THE GAME I II III IV V VI
Playa Ray
SLAUGHTER GANG I II III
RUTHLESS HEART I II III
By Willie Slaughter
FUK SHYT
By Blakk Diamond
DON'T F#CK WITH MY HEART I II
By Linnea
ADDICTED TO THE DRAMA I II III
IN THE ARM OF HIS BOSS II
By Jamila
YAYO I II III IV
A SHOOTER'S AMBITION I II
BRED IN THE GAME
By S. Allen

TRAP GOD I II III

RICH $AVAGE

MONEY IN THE GRAVE I II III

By Martell Troublesome Bolden

FOREVER GANGSTA

GLOCKS ON SATIN SHEETS I II

By Adrian Dulan

TOE TAGZ I II III IV

LEVELS TO THIS SHYT I II

By Ah'Million

KINGPIN DREAMS I II III

By Paper Boi Rari

CONFESSIONS OF A GANGSTA I II III IV

CONFESSIONS OF A JACKBOY I II

By Nicholas Lock

I'M NOTHING WITHOUT HIS LOVE

SINS OF A THUG

TO THE THUG I LOVED BEFORE

A GANGSTA SAVED XMAS

IN A HUSTLER I TRUST

By Monet Dragun

CAUGHT UP IN THE LIFE I II III

THE STREETS NEVER LET GO

By Robert Baptiste

NEW TO THE GAME I II III

MONEY, MURDER & MEMORIES I II III

By **Malik D. Rice**

LIFE OF A SAVAGE I II III

A GANGSTA'S QUR'AN I II III IV

MURDA SEASON I II III

GANGLAND CARTEL I II III

CHI'RAQ GANGSTAS I II III

KILLERS ON ELM STREET I II III

JACK BOYZ N DA BRONX I II III

A DOPEBOY'S DREAM I II III

JACK BOYS VS DOPE BOYS

By **Romell Tukes**

LOYALTY AIN'T PROMISED I II

By Keith Williams

QUIET MONEY I II III

THUG LIFE I II III

EXTENDED CLIP I II

By **Trai'Quan**

THE STREETS MADE ME I II III

By **Larry D. Wright**

THE ULTIMATE SACRIFICE I, II, III, IV, V, VI

KHADIFI

IF YOU CROSS ME ONCE

ANGEL I II

IN THE BLINK OF AN EYE

By **Anthony Fields**

THE LIFE OF A HOOD STAR

By Ca$h & Rashia Wilson

THE STREETS WILL NEVER CLOSE I II

By K'ajji

CREAM I II

By Yolanda Moore

NIGHTMARES OF A HUSTLA I II III

By King Dream

CONCRETE KILLA I II

VICIOUS LOYALTY

By Kingpen

HARD AND RUTHLESS I II

MOB TOWN 251

THE BILLIONAIRE BENTLEYS I II

By Von Diesel

GHOST MOB

Stilloan Robinson

MOB TIES I II III IV V

By SayNoMore

BODYMORE MURDERLAND I II III

By Delmont Player

FOR THE LOVE OF A BOSS

By C. D. Blue

MOBBED UP I II III IV

THE BRICK MAN I II III

THE COCAINE PRINCESS I II

By King Rio

KILLA KOUNTY I II

By Khufu

MONEY GAME I II

By Smoove Dolla

A GANGSTA'S KARMA I II

By FLAME

KING OF THE TRENCHES I II

by **GHOST & TRANAY ADAMS**

QUEEN OF THE ZOO

By **Black Migo**

GRIMEY WAYS

By Ray Vinci

XMAS WITH AN ATL SHOOTER

By Ca$h & Destiny Skai

KING KILLA

By Vincent "Vitto" Holloway

BOOKS BY LDP'S CEO, CA$H

TRUST IN NO MAN

TRUST IN NO MAN 2

TRUST IN NO MAN 3

BONDED BY BLOOD

SHORTY GOT A THUG

THUGS CRY

THUGS CRY 2

THUGS CRY 3

TRUST NO BITCH

TRUST NO BITCH 2

TRUST NO BITCH 3

TIL MY CASKET DROPS

RESTRAINING ORDER

RESTRAINING ORDER 2

IN LOVE WITH A CONVICT

LIFE OF A HOOD STAR

XMAS WITH AN ATL SHOOTER

Money in the Grave 3